WARNING!
Cute
Kid Stories
Ahead!

WARNING!
Cute
Kid Stories
Ahead!

A Bulletin Board Collection

Edited by Daniel Kelly

PIONEER BOOKS

ANDREWS AND McMEEL
A Universal Press Syndicate Company
Kansas City

Additional copies of this book may be ordered by calling (800) 642-6480.

Library of Congress Cataloging-in-Publication Data
Warning! cute kid stories ahead! : a Bulletin board collection /
    edited by Daniel Kelly.
        p. cm. — (Pioneer books)
    ISBN 0-8362-0585-5 (pbk.)
    1. Children—Humor. 2. Family—Humor. I. Kelly, Daniel.
II. Bulletin Board (St. Paul, Minn.) III. Series: Pioneer books
(Kansas City, Mo.)
PN6231.C32W37 1995
818'.5402080352054—dc20   95-23627
                                                               CIP

PIONEER BOOKS

Contents

Foreword

I happen to love children, in (virtually) all of their guises: innocent and mischievous, sweet and sassy, naive and wise.

So it was easy for me to ignore **Mark** of Oakdale.

Longtime Bulletin Boarders will recall that after we'd published just a few cute kid stories on the Bulletin Board page of the St. Paul Pioneer Press, Mark of Oakdale was the Grumpy Gus who warned us, in the sternest terms, to cease and desist with such folly:

"I almost called right away to nip it in the bud when you first devoted the entire Bulletin Board to the pleasures of childedness, or whatever you call it. But I refrained. Let a few puffed-up parents have their day, I thought. But now these sappy stories are popping up every day in your column.

"I'm warning you: Stop it before it gets out of control. Pretty soon you'll be inundated with calls from irate parents who, if you don't run the story about their cute kid, will be complaining 'til hell freezes over. Their kid, of course, does and says things far cuter than the ones you've included in the column. Parental one-upmanship knows no bounds."

Mark was dead wrong, of course. Thousands upon thousands of Bulletin Boarders have since called to tell stories about their own kids and others'—with complaints and one-upmanship being conspicuously absent. (Even so, Mark's tirade wasn't utterly worthless. He did, after all, inspire our standard caveat, "WARNING! Cute kids stories ahead!"—which has become the title of this book. Take a bow, Mark.)

Several dozen of the best stories about children made it into our first book, *The Best of Bulletin Board*. You'll find several hundred more of them here. I hope I've chosen well.

And if I have, please know that much credit must go to my sister Maureen Nalezny, who read and offered fresh verdicts on the vast collection of cute kid stories that have found their way into Bulletin Board. (My 11-year-old niece, Megan, also read the entire inventory—but she liked all of them. Now *there's* a cute kid.) Maureen's guidance was invaluable.

So was that of my wife, Patty, who became, while this collection too slowly came together, a single mother to our girls, Laura and Rose—who, by the way, love to hear these stories read aloud. (Try it. Read them out loud—even if you're reading just to yourself. They improve, I think, with volume.)

My greatest thanks must go, as always, to the readers of the Pioneer Press—without whom Bulletin Board does not exist.

D.K.

Grandma Dottie of St. Paul: "My son and his family were over on Sunday. My two grandsons were playing cards—and, like most kids, the boys started fighting. So their dad told them to put the cards away.

"The 6-year-old kept saying he wanted the cards; his dad kept saying no. So the 6-year-old went into the kitchen and came back with a note and gave it to his dad. The note said:

" 'Dear Dad,

" 'I hate you.

" 'Love, Luke.' "

Sergeant Sue of Apple Valley: "I had to have three wisdom teeth pulled out this week. Not much fun. I got home, and I was lying on the couch trying to rest.

"My 6-year-old son, Jesse, was busy in his bedroom for a few minutes and then came out and said: 'I have a present for you, Mom.'

"I was in some pain at the moment, so I said: 'Just put it down here.' I was dozing.

"About an hour later, he yanked on my sleeve and said: 'Can you open your present now?'

"I said: 'OK, honey, I'll open it.' He had wrapped it up in his bathrobe, and he had put a little note he wrote in the pocket, so he said: 'Read the note first.'

"So I pulled the note out, and it said: 'I love you, Mom. From Jesse.' And I opened up the bathrobe, and inside was his teddy bear.

"He said: 'I want to give you my teddy bear. That'll help you feel better.'

"I thought that was something really sweet for a 6-year-old boy to think of, all by himself, in his room, while his mom was lying on the couch trying to rest from having three teeth pulled out earlier that day."

BULLETIN BOARD ADDS: There was a bit of a sniffle in Sergeant Sue's report, right there at the end. And no wonder.

What a nice boy.

Jean of Red Wing: "My son, who is 5, was talking about how much he loves his little sister, Natalie, who is 2.

"He said: 'Oh, Mom, I really love Natalie. She is so cute, and I just love her so much. And, you know, she's almost like part of the family now!' "

Sheila of South St. Paul: "On Mother's Day, I was snuggling with my 6-year-old daughter, talking about how happy I was to be her mom. She asked me when I became a mom. I said: 'Oh, I'll never forget that day; it was March 28th, 1987.'

"Her eyes got really big, and she said: 'I don't believe it, Mom! That's the exact-same day as my birthday!'

"I thought it was really sweet; she still doesn't get it."

Terri of Cottage Grove: "My daughter Tracy is 7 years old. She joined a book club, and she just got her first package today. It was in the door when we got home.

"She picked it up—she was so excited—and she said: 'I've been waiting *four to six weeks* for this!' "

The Reading Doc of Rochester: "When my daughter Kathy was in her late teens, she was a counselor at a riding camp/ranch. Although the days were pretty structured most of the time, the first afternoon was free time.

"One little 8-year-old, Libby, asked Kathy what there was to do. Kathy told her that she could play tennis, go swimming or go canoeing. Or, she could even go bareback riding if she wanted to give it a try.

" 'Really?' asked Libby.

" 'Sure,' said Kathy. 'You'll like it.'

" 'Well, OK,' said Libby. 'Where are the bears?' "

Ladine of Ellsworth, Wis.: "We had raised some beef cattle. We were getting ready to sell them. We sold them for butcher, and my 3-year-old daughter asked my father-in-law where the cows went.

"Well, we didn't have the heart to tell her where, exactly, they went, so he told her they went to market.

"A couple days later, someone asked her what happened to our cows.

"She said: 'They went shopping.'"

Gaga of River Falls, Wis.: "When my grandson was 3, he was sitting on my front porch eating a Popsicle. Several bees started coming out from under the lights, so I said: 'Honey, why don't you go stand by the garage while I spray these bees? The spray wouldn't be too good for you.'

"He did, and I sprayed the light area; about 20 bees dropped dead on the porch. He stood licking his Popsicle and watching, and he said: 'It's not too good for the bees, either, Gaga.'"

Dave M. of Cottage Grove: "We were up at the cabin last weekend, sittin' out by the bonfire. I have a son, Jason, who's 6, and a daughter, Emily, who's 5. Jason picks up a piece of birch bark, and it's got an an ant on it; he looks at it and says: 'You're goin' in the fire, ant.' Tosses it in there, right in the middle of this huge blaze.

"My daughter looks at it real deadpan and says: 'Stop, drop and roll, ant.'"

Jill of Eagan: "My brother asked his first-grader what he would do if a stranger came up and offered him a ride.

"Tyler quickly and confidently responded: 'Stop, drop and roll!'"
BULLETIN BOARD NOTES: Beats getting in the car.

Jan of Cottage Grove: "Our 5-year-old neighbor is such a delight—a real talker. She was talking, at length, with my husband, Ray, one day and concluded with: 'Ray, you're my best friend.'

"Well, we thought that was so nice—but we were sure she has many best friends.

"Several days later, as she and I were walking hand-in-hand, she looked up at me and said: 'Jan, I like you—but Ray is my best friend.'"

Barb of St. Paul: "My aunt is a great gardener. One year, she had a bumper crop of cucumbers. She's always real generous with her produce.

"She sent a sackful home with the little boy next door, who peeked into the bag and said: 'Oh, good. My mom likes these small ones. They're easier to put down the garbage disposer.'"

Marjorie of Hastings: "My granddaughter and I were planting bulbs in the garden—and it occurred to me that maybe she'd like to stay for dinner.

"She said: 'Grandma, what are you having?'

"I said: 'Pot roast. Carrots and potatoes.'

"She said: 'Well, Grandma, I think I'll call Mommy up and find out what we're having for supper.'

"So she calls, and then she says: 'Grandma, we're having pizza. I think I'll go home and have a decent meal.'"

Marge of St. Paul: "My oldest sister has an 8-year-old who isn't used to having a mother home to cook. She happens to be the Queen of Domino's Pizza.

"He was over at a friend's house in the neighborhood, and it turns out that they were making all kinds of treats. He came home and told his mother: 'Mom, these people are so weird. Did you know that you can make cake at home?'"

Jeanne of St. Paul—talking about her neighbor: "When she was raising the kids, there was not a lot of money. Hamburger and meatloaf were the usual menu.

"One day, she bought some pork chops. She had them on the counter, ready to be cooked. Her son came in and asked what they were.

"She said: 'They're pork chops!'

"He said: 'When did they start making *those*?'"

The Senator of Hayward, Wis.: "Actually, I'm a retired schoolteacher. My wife just calls me Senator because she says she can never get a straight answer from me.

"My favorite classroom story concerns a young third-grade girl who came to school one morning all excited. She explained that things were really different at their house now because her grandfather had come to live with them. Then, she said: 'And he's sterile, you know.'

"The teacher thought for a moment and then replied: 'You mean senile, don't you?'

"The child replied: 'That, too.'

"Art Linkletter was right. Kids do say the darnedest things. And often, too."

Michelle Reuther of Lake Elmo: "My daughter, who has the most healthy self-esteem of anyone I know, came home from kindergarten one day last fall and told me that she'd made a new friend on the bus.

"I said: 'That's really nice, honey. What's her name?'

"And she replied: 'I don't know, but she's so beautiful she could be my sister.'"

Iowa of parts undisclosed: "I wish that I could have my 2-year-old's optimistic view of life. No matter what is happening, he can always find something fun and exciting.

"Yesterday, he woke up with a cold. We were snuggling together, and I was listening to his labored breathing, thinking: 'Oh, poor little guy.'

"He looked up at me with a big smile and said: 'Listen to me purr, Mom!'"

R.C. of Highland Park: "About a week ago, my 2½-year-old had strep throat, and I'd been giving him his penicillin with a dropper-type medicine dispenser.

"The other day, when I was making a turkey, I set him on the kitchen counter to give him his medicine, and he took a look at the turkey baster, and his eyes got really big, and he says to me: 'That's for my *medicine*?'"

Gramma Barb of St. Paul: "A couple of days ago, my granddaughter Nicole, age 2½, was taken to urgent care by her mommy and daddy—'cause there was a possible urinary infection.

"Upon leaving the office, Nicole surprised the lady doctor by saying: 'Thanks for checkin' my butt!'"

Franci of Eau Claire, Wis.: "We're always trying to impress upon our kids the importance of personal hygiene.

"About a year ago, I caught our 4-year-old, Sam, with his hand down the back of his pants, and when I told him that he needed to go wash his hands, he responded with: 'It's all right, Mom! I don't need to wash my hands. I was only scratchin' the mountain, not the line!'"

A.R. of Hudson: "A few weeks ago, before the first frost, my 2-year-old daughter came running to me and said her 3-year-old brother had bit her.

"I said: 'Did you bite your sister?'

"And he said: 'No, mom, I was just scratching her mosquito bites with my teeth.'"

J.B. of White Bear Lake: "I was home in South Dakota recently, and my dad was telling me about a friend of our family, a first-grader, who went in for her first confession.

"The priest told her to say two Hail Marys, and she came out looking very, very sad. Her mom asked her what was the matter, and she said: 'He said to say two Hail Marys, but I only know one.'"

Jan of Woodbury: "We were in Barnes & Noble the other night, and a little 3-year-old child was crying, and the mother very sternly said: 'You . . . stop . . . that . . . crying . . . right . . . now.'

"And the child, continuing to cry, says: 'But I . . . don't . . . know . . . how . . . to!'"

Dr. Bob of St. Paul: "This is from a long time ago: My little brother was about 4 years old; we were riding in the car, being completely obnoxious in the back seat, and my dad screams at us: 'Act your age!'

"My little brother leans up to me and, with great comic timing, stage-whispers: 'Bob! How old *am* I?'"

Another Mom of Eagan: "Last Saturday, we were at Macy's shopping, and when we were in the dressing room, the woman next door was evidently trying on a dress for an upcoming wedding when her son or daughter said: 'Hey, Mom, are you gonna put socks in your bra for this one, too?'

"My mom and I had a hard time keeping ourselves quiet."

Grandma Visiting From Florida: "Our 4-year-old grandson went to the playground, accompanied by his father. Chris had to go to the bathroom, so his dad took him over to the one portable john, where there was a line.

"After fidgeting awhile, Chris said: 'Dad, I really gotta go.'

" 'Chris,' Dad said, 'you'll just have to wait, because there's a guy in there.'

"And Chris, in his extra-loud voice, said, 'Hey guy! You got the diarrhea?' "

Sue of Oakdale: "I have a 3-year-old girl named Amy. We were standing in line at an elementary school, waiting to vote on a referendum for our school district, and she was being a good 3-year-old, and she asked if she could go play on the mats with the other children.

"I told her no—that I didn't know those other kids, and I wanted her to stay in line with me.

"So, being the good 3-year-old she is, she promptly faced forward and stood in line. I was watching her, and I realized that she was butt-level . . . or face-level, or however you want to put it—to the man in front of her.

"She was looking directly at his butt—and suddenly she started leaning forward, and she was about an inch away from this man's butt. And she starts sniffing!

"And I'm standing there in horror, thinking: What is my daughter doing? She's sniffing, and she's sniffing, and she turns her little head around and says: 'Hey, Mom!'

"I said: 'What?'

"And she says: 'Come here.'

"So now I bend over, and I'm now face-level with this man's butt, and she says: 'Smell this guy's butt!'

"How would you respond?"

BULLETIN BOARD RESPONDS: "We don't sniff other people's butts, Amy. Our own, either."

Next question?

Joan of West St. Paul: "When my daughter was about 3½ years old, we were standing in line for Tiny Tim doughnuts at Como Zoo. I was chatting with the lady in line behind me, and all of a sudden, my daughter starts screaming, 'Lady! Lady! Lady!'—real alarmed-like.

"I stopped and said: 'What . . . is . . . the *matter*?'

"The woman in front of us turns around, and my daughter gets a real serious look on her face. She goes: 'Lady, you have a fly on your butt.' "

Mary of Vadnais Heights: "I was strolling through Como Park yesterday with my 10-month-old daughter, and we were just about to go into the primate building—and right at the entrance, there's this life-size metal statue of a gorilla.

"And as we were walking past it, another woman with a baby in a stroller and a little boy, who was about 3, were walking past it, too. And this little boy walks up to the statue, slowly pats the side of this gorilla, and with a really serious face, he looks back at his mom and in kind of a hushed voice, he says: 'Mom, I think this one's dead.' "

J.D. of Woodbury: "The first day of fourth grade, my daughter brought home a worksheet that had a lot of fill-in-the-blanks on it.

"It was kind of a description of All About Me. It had blanks to fill in: My parents' names are so-and-so, and my brothers and sisters are so-and-so.

"She proceeded to fill in the entire worksheet. Down at the bottom, it said: 'My pets are . . . '—and she filled in: 'Dead.' Both the turtle and the cat had died the previous spring.

"We thought it was a hoot, and we saved it in her permanent file."

Nancy P. of parts undisclosed: "Two years ago, my son, then 6 years old, was honored with the job of caring for Brownie, the class hamster, during the summer. We all became quite attached to this creature.

"Today, my son told us at bedtime: 'I have bad news. Brownie is dead.' After some conversation on death, I explained that Brownie probably went to heaven.

"My 4-year-old, in the lower bunk and in deep thought on the subject, remembered a dead squirrel we came across at Wisconsin Dells last summer and said: 'I think the squirrel is in heaven.'

"My 8-year-old, from the upper bunk, says: 'How many heavens are there?'

"I replied that I thought there was only one.

"He then said, even more seriously: 'I don't want to be in the same heaven as that dead squirrel.'"

Bushwhacker Steve of Blaine: "We have to drive three hours each way to pick my children up from where they live with their mom, and occasionally we play a game called 'I'm Thinking Of.'

"This is a game in which one of us thinks of something a certain color, and the other people have to guess what it is. For example: If I say 'I'm thinking of something green,' they say: 'Grass.'

"Well, being little kids, they are kind of obsessed about certain bodily functions, so we try to avoid brown and yellow, when possible.

"It was my turn a couple weeks ago—and, not thinking clearly, I thought of a lemon. I said: 'I'm thinking of something yellow'—and immediately my younger daughter chimed in with 'Pee!'

"Disgustedly, I said: 'No, it's not pee.'

"And then she said: 'Well, is it *deer* pee, Dad?'

"She looked at her sister and said: 'Oh, maybe it's squirrel pee.'

"I think we're going to have to change this game totally. I don't think it's going to work anymore."

Nubbins of St. Paul: "Here's one of those precious moments with my daughter that left me quite without an answer.

"At bedtime one night after a great weekend at the cabin during which we spent copious amounts of time outdoors tracking deer and generally communing with nature, my 5-year-old daughter, Maggie, popped the big question: 'Mommy, when deers pee and poop in the woods, do they squint?'"

Ellen of Stillwater: "My 6-year-old son for the first time had a friend overnight. They were settled in the same bed, all tucked in, both heads on the same pillow, when my son turned to his friend and said: 'Do you wet?'"

Mamarama of South St. Paul: "My son and I have had the usual routine of getting ready for bed: getting jammies on, brushing teeth, a good-night story, a hug and a kiss ... and we call it a night.

"Tonight, I turned out the light and said: 'Good night, Sweet Pea.'

"He said: 'Good night, Sweet Poop.' "

Mother of Many of West St. Paul: "My sister had a little boy over—she was baby-sitting—and he was playing with the Nativity figures and put one of the shepherds out back behind the stable.

"We asked him why the shepherd was there—and if he was coming later. And he told us: 'No. He's out there peeing.' "

Lorraine of North St. Paul: "My granddaughter Jennifer, who's 4 years old and lives in Lake Elmo, was playing with her mother's Nativity scene before Christmas and had all of the characters lined up inside the stable—except she left one outside.

"Her mother asked her what that one was doing outside, and she said: 'He's taking tickets.' "

Grandma Jones of Columbia Heights: "My 4-year-old granddaughter loves playing with the figurines of our Nativity set. I had told her the story, stressing their joy and celebration on the night Jesus was born.

"Later, noting that she had all of the characters lined up in a processional arrangement, I asked if they were waiting in line to see the baby Jesus.

" 'No, Grandma,' she said. 'They're doing the bunny hop.' "

Bonnie of West St. Paul: "Jordan, age 4, my imaginative granddaughter, was playing with the Christmas creche—talking to the figures and moving them about.

"In passing, I said: 'And what is the baby Jesus doing tonight?'

"Innocently, she replied: 'He's with a sitter. Mary and Joseph are out for the evening.' "

BULLETIN BOARD REPLIES: Let's hope they made reservations. Places get pretty booked up at Christmastime.

Fiamma of Forest Lake: "When I was a first-grade art teacher, one of the classes was a group of children who were obviously not as well off as some of the other kiddos. They'd been put together in this one room because the teacher was this especially nice teacher; she really was very understanding.

"Anyway, this one little girl that you just wanted to take home and feed for about four years—she looked so skinny; little scraggly blonde—had drawn this really nice little picture. This was about Christmastime, and you could see Mary, and you could see Joseph and the shepherds—but when you looked closely, you could see that Joseph had this humongous frown on this face.

"I said: 'Well, Shirley, what's the matter with Joseph?'

"And she said: 'Mary just told him they're gonna have another baby.'"

Cindy of Mahtomedi: "We set out our creche for the holidays, and my 3-year-old daughter, Laura, was watching me put all of the figurines in it—especially the baby Jesus.

"I explained what a manger was—that they didn't have a crib for him, so they had to lay a blanket on the hay and put him there. She thought about that for a minute, and then she looked at me and said: 'Mom, did they have to use the manger for his car seat, too?'"

Dennis of Circle Pines: "The other day, my wife and I and our daughter got in the car to go somewhere. My daughter is 6 years old, and she's real religious about buckling her seat belt.

"As we were backing out the driveway and I put the car in Forward to go down the road, my daughter kinda leaned over and says: 'Mom and Dad! Aren't you gonna buckle your seat belt? If we get in an accident and you fly through the windshield, who's gonna drive me home?'

"It's kinda funny when a 6-year-old is smarter than you are."

Janet of Shoreview: "Driving down Lexington Avenue, I stopped as an ambulance and two police cars raced by. My 4-year-old daughter, in the back seat, says: 'Poor Humpy-Dumpy fell off the wall!'

"And my 5-year-old daughter, who was also sitting back there, shouts out: 'Well, he shouldn't have been sitting there in the first place.'"

Dawn of St. Paul: "My son had to go to the hospital and have stitches in his forehead. He's 4 years old, and he's lying on the table, screaming like crazy.

"All of a sudden, he caught a glimpse of the little hook that they stitch you up with, and he yells: 'Hey, put that down! You could hurt somebody with that!' "

Gramma Judie of Stillwater: "The other day, my 3-year-old granddaughter, Sara, and I were cleaning my bathroom.

"Sara came upon a thermometer, and I said to her: 'Please don't break that, sweetie-pie.'

"Her reply to me was: 'Don't worry, Gramma. I'm a Be Careful girl.'

"Isn't she a doll?"

BULLETIN BOARD REPLIES: No doubt. So, for our money, is Gramma.

Kelly Eder of Lake Elmo: "I have two daughters, Alyssa and Nicole, who adore their aunt 'Auntie.' Auntie is very tall, very blonde, very vivacious and very beautiful, and she allows the girls to do as they wish when she is around.

"Auntie was baby-sitting the girls and tucking them in for the night. Nicole said to her, 'Auntie, I wish I were just like you.' Auntie was feeling a special wave of love and adoration when Nicole then added: 'Then I could reach the stuff on my dresser.' "

Princess Grace of Mahtomedi: "I've often thought that it would be wonderful if we parents had an audience that would sit there and clap for us when we do something really good.

"Last night, I was having a little talk with my daughter; there were some things we needed to clarify about behavior and things, and she was just contemplating me really gravely the whole time I was talking, really paying attention.

"I finished, and she was silent, and I was mentally congratulating myself for doing a wonderful job; would've been nice to hear that applause.

"And my daughter suddenly said to me: 'Mom, what's that mark on your face?' That's what she had been looking at the whole time.

"Just one of those things that bring you down to earth and keep you humble."

Kathy of Coon Rapids: "I was just giving my 3-year-old a bath. I'm looking down at her as I'm washing her hair and feeling all sorts of motherly love for that beautiful little face.

"I said to her: 'Anna, you have the prettiest little face.'

"And she said: 'You have boogers up your nose.'"

Mark of Woodbury: "I've got a 5½-year-old son, Michael, who's a pretty cool kid.

"We do things for each other, like scratch each other's backs, and sometimes we'll reach over and sorta rub each other's arm or hand with the fingernails. It kinda tickles, and it feels really good.

"One day, he and I are out doing errands in the car, and my arm is on the arm rest, and he reaches over and starts rubbin' the back of my hand, ticklin' it, up and down my arm a little bit, under my sleeve.

"I said: 'Michael, that feels really good. That's really nice of you to do that. Thank you; that's really nice.'

"He smiles at me.

"About 10 minutes later, after all I've been doin' is thinkin' how nice a kid he is, he says: 'Dad?'

"I said: 'What, Michael?'

"He says: 'Remember when I tickled your arm and you told me how nice I was?'

"I said: 'Yeah. That *was* really nice.'

"He says: 'Well, I didn't do that just to be nice.'

"I said: 'You didn't? What did you do that for, then?'

"He smiled that great smile he's got, and he says: 'I slid a booger up your sleeve.'

"True story.

"I still think he's a cool kid."

Weas of the Midway: "My 4-year-old, when asked if she knew what nostrils were, said: 'Yeah. These holes in your nose that you put your fingers in.'"

Michelle of Woodbury: "My 2-year-old daughter, Amanda, was talking to her grandfather on the phone yesterday, and he asked her: 'What are you doing right now, Amanda?'

"She very honestly said: 'I'm picking my nose.' "

Leslie of parts undisclosed: "My dog, Beast from Hell—well, actually it's Charlie—accompanies me to the office every day.

"One morning, a young woman with a toddler came into the office. Charlie ambled over to the youngster to get a proper whiff of his diaper (it's a dog thing, you know), and the little kid shoved his finger straight up the dog's nose.

"Yikes! Both mom and I were speechless (and terrified), and she reached out for the kid's hand and withdrew the offending finger.

"Mom said: 'You don't do that to your *own* nose!'

"To which the little kid responded: 'Yes, I do.' "

Debi of Roseville: "Last week, my 5-year-old son, David, and I were taking our dog, Darby, to the vet for her check-up. On the way there, Darby was jumping around in the car, and suddenly David said: 'Oooh! Darby jumped on my penis!'

"I answered back, sympathetically: 'Oh! How did *that* feel?'

"Whereupon David replied: 'Hmmm . . . pretty good!' "

Margaret of Minneapolis: "I gave my 3-year-old niece a pre-school language exam, just for practice (I'm studying speech/language therapy at school). One series of questions probed how well she understood the function of various body parts.

"I asked: 'What do you hear with?' And she pointed to her ears.

"I asked: 'What do you see with?' And she pointed to her eyes.

"And: 'What do you smell with?' And she very solemnly pointed to her bottom."

BULLETIN BOARD REPLIES: So, three for three!

Katie of Stillwater: "A couple of years ago, when my two boys were about 4 and 5, they were always getting out of control, so it wasn't uncommon for them to hear me yell, 'Quiet! I can't hear myself think!'

"One night, my son Lucas came downstairs when I was making dinner, and he said: 'Mom! What's that *smell*?'

"And I said: 'Dinner.'

"And he said: 'Ooooh. It really smells strong. Mommy, that smell's so strong I can't smell myself think!'

"Kids. Gotta love 'em."

Anonymous Mom of Stillwater: "My son is about to turn 6, and we were talking about what kind of birthday party he should have this year—and he said he wanted to go to Discovery Zone.

"Now, since he's never been to Discovery Zone, I wasn't sure why he chose that. But my older daughter had been there, so I said: 'Tell us about Discovery Zone. What's it like?'

"She said: 'Oh, it's *so . . . noisy* at Discovery Zone. You can't even hear yourself think.'

"My son said: 'Well, then that's perfect—because I don't *like* to think.'"

Sharon Lee of Shoreview: "When my brother-in-law's younger son was, oh, somewhere between 3 and 5, he acted up at the dinner table and was sent away. When he was allowed to come back to the table, his father asked him: 'Now, are you properly repentant?'

"David gave the only honest answer he could. He said: 'No.'"

Paul Johnston of St. Paul: "My son recently turned 5, so my wife, Sarah, was sitting with him last night at the table, and they were writing thank-you notes. She was writing; he was signing his name and doing little bits of artwork. And they got to my Aunt Lynne, who'd sent him a check.

"Sarah said: 'Now, Peter, what do you want to say to Lynne?'

"And he said: 'Dear Aunt Lynne, I love you.'

"She said: 'Well, you have to say more than that.'

"So he said: 'Dear Aunt Lynne, I love your money.'

"At least the kid's honest."

Sally of North St. Paul: "My nephew, Adam, just turned 6. He called me to invite me to his birthday party. This is the gist of our conversation:

"Adam: 'Would you like to come to my birthday party?'

"I answered: 'Yes, Adam, I'd love to.'

"Kelly, Adam's mom, in the background: 'Adam, tell her she doesn't have to bring a present.'

"Long pause.

"Kelly, in the background: 'Adam, tell her we just want her company, and she doesn't have to bring a present.'

"Another pause.

"Adam, into the phone: 'Uh, you only have to bring one present.'"

Tar Heel Neil of St. Paul: "You don't have to caution me that there's a cute kid story ahead; I think the kid stories are great—because kids haven't been polluted yet by adult civilization.

"This one is from Steven, age 9, who was told to write his grandfather, who had sent him a $5 bill for Christmas. He did, at his mother's insistence, and he wrote: 'Dear Grandpa, I received your $5 bill for Christmas, and I thank you more than enough.'

"We still say that in our family, at times: 'I thank you more than enough.'"

Dick of Maplewood: "My daughter had this Jump-Rope-A-Thon at school—and, of course, she forgot to go out and get pledges.

"Frantically, on Wednesday morning, she said: 'I forgot to do my pledges!'

"And I said: 'Don't worry. I'll write some pledge names down here.'

"So I write my name down, and I put down $5, and I write Grandpa's name down and put $2, and I write Grandma's name and put $2, and I write Uncle Tom's name and put down $1. I figured: Well, $10 is enough to get her into this Jump-Rope-A-Thon; I put that into the envelope with all of these names and how much they contributed.

"And she looks at this thing and says: 'You mean Uncle Tom only gave us *one...dollar*?'"

Mom of St. Paul: "Yesterday was my 38th birthday. It was kind of a bittersweet one, because I'm in the middle of a divorce. But my kids went to the dollar store to buy me some birthday presents, and they were so happy when they came home because they'd picked out the presents all by themselves.

"I have to tell you what they bought me. They bought me deodorant and mouthwash."

Jill of St. Paul: "Last night, my little girls—who are ages 6 and 3½—were playing Power Rangers. My little one is particularly a prissy type; she is always wearing a dress.

"The older one says: 'Let's play Power Rangers and fight the forces of evil!'

"And my little one says: 'Just a minute. I have to get my purse.'"

Grandma L. of Stillwater: "My two grandsons were over, and I gave them each a colored marker to circle toys they would like in the catalogs that have come through the mail. And the 7-year-old, along with circling X-Men and trucks, circled the credit cards in the corner of the page.

"He's a pretty smart little kid."

City Girl of Stillwater: "Ever since we bought a farm, our little tomboy has been begging for a horse. We've agreed to get her one, when we think she's ready.

"So the other day, the 7-year-old and I are discussing possible names. And she starts rattling off her choices: Black, White . . . VISA Card.

"VISA Card?

"Whoa! Guess she knows more about horses than I thought."

Connie of St. Paul: "My 2½-year-old son was shaking his Christmas presents about a week ago. It was a puzzle inside, but he obviously didn't know that yet.

"He's shaking it, and he says: 'Mom, what's in there?' I said: 'I don't know, honey. What do you think it is?'

"He's shaking it, and he's got a real serious look on his face, and suddenly his eyes light up and his face brightens up and he says: 'It's rocks!'

"He thought it was rocks—and he was happy as heck. He was just thrilled that he was getting a box of rocks.

"So I obviously bought the wrong gift for him."

Judy of the East Side, who called, late at night, when she was thinking about the amusements her son—just about to turn 6— had provided her:

"When my son was 4, his aunt was having a baby, and he wanted to know how the baby came out. He said: 'Does the baby bite its way and claw its way out?'

"And just this spring, he saw a big boulder in someone's yard, and he looked at me real seriously and said: 'How big do rocks *get*?'

"He gets so mad when he asks these questions that make me laugh—but I can't help it. It's only because I love him so much."

Crabby of St. Paul Park: "But I'm not crabby anymore; I have got the best little-kid story for ya:

"I'm comin' home. Just got ripped off at the department store. Had a real terrible day at work.

"Drivin' home down Summit Avenue, I see three tiny little kids tryin' to be little entrepreneurs, sellin' stuff. I think they're sellin' lemonade.

"They're selling . . . rocks. The cutest.

"We stop, and they say: 'The big one is 10 cents. The little one is 5 cents.' We couldn't help but give 'em the rest of the money we had in our pockets. They're trying to save up for a remote-control car.

"They were just the cutest. Made my whole day."

Goggy of White Bear: "One day while he was looking in my purse, my 5-year-old grandson, Zachary, asked me in a plaintive voice: 'Can I have some money?'

"I questioned him: 'What for?'

"His face lit up as he exclaimed, in a matter-of-fact tone: 'I collect it!' "

BULLETIN BOARD REPLIES: Get in line, lad.

The Polarfleece Lady of Maplewood: "Several years ago, I was driving my 5-year-old son and two of his friends to a birthday party.

"As we passed 3M on I-94, one of the boys exclaimed: 'That's where my daddy works. He makes tape.'

"The second boy announced: 'My daddy works there, too. He makes glue.'

"My son sat quietly in the back seat for a few moments—and then said: 'Well, my daddy works for the phone company, and he makes *money*.' "

Holly of St. Paul: "I had taken my 3-year-old son, Bryant, to the St. Paul Saints' game. There were two girls sitting behind us, both about 7 years old, and they were talking about their grandmas and all of the wonderful things they do.

"One of the girls said: 'My grandma makes special quilts and sells them to people.'

"And the other girl said: 'Well, *my* grandma works in a hospital and takes care of sick people—you know, real important stuff.'

"My son—my wonderful 3-year-old—decided to invite himself into the conversation and say: 'Well, *my* grandma makes macaroni and cheese!'"

Rosella of South St. Paul: "I took my grandsons to the cemetery where their grandfather is buried. My 9-year-old grandson wanted to know why there was a carving of a tree on the monument.

"I said: 'Grandpa liked trees.'

"He looked at some of the other stones and said: 'This one must have liked flowers' and 'This one liked to pray.'

"And then with a very serious look on his face, he said: 'I think I'd like macaroni and cheese on mine.'"

Justice of Mahtomedi: "I was making macaroni and cheese for my 5-year-old cousin, and I had her try one of the noodles to see if it was done. It was crunchy; it wasn't quite done. She looked at me with a weird look on her face and said: 'I don't like the kinds with bones in 'em.'"

Donna of West St. Paul: "My niece Laura was eating a peanut butter sandwich one day, and it happened to be crunchy peanut butter. She turns to her mom and says: 'Mom, I don't like peanut butter with bones in it.'"

Kay of Lutsen: "After I returned from grocery shopping one day, my 5-year-old daughter, Ashley, wanted to know what kind of breakfast cereal I'd brought home. This trip, I'd vowed to avoid 'Sugar Twinkles' and 'Chockfull of Calories' and opted for a healthier selection.

"I showed her the box, and she groaned: 'Yuck! What's in it?'

"'Toenails and raisins,' I said.

"Nearly in tears, she said: 'But Mom, I *hate* raisins!'"

Terri of St. Paul: "My 2½-year-old daughter and I just finished baking up the best batch of chocolate chip cookies that we've ever tasted.

"I said: 'Gee, these must be the best chocolate chip cookies I've ever eaten. I hope they're good for us.'

"She said: 'Yeah, they're good for us! They've got *chocolate* in 'em!'"

A Mom of the Midway: "Those things that get in the corner of your eyes? I think somebody called 'em *eye boogers*; we call 'em *sleepies*. Well anyway, my daughter told me that sleepies taste like chocolate, and I said: 'Euugh! Gross!'

"And she said: 'But Mom, you *like* chocolate.'

"I'm going to miss having a 4-year-old in the house. She's the younger of two and probably will not have any younger brothers or sisters. She's such a fountain of whimsy; we just enjoy her very much."

Red Fox of Spooner, Wis.: "The first time my nephew went fishing with his grandfather, the young lad caught a nice-size fish, and he watched closely while his Grampa showed him how to clean it. He watched as Gramma explained how to bread and fry the fillet.

"When dinnertime came and his plate was filled with the catch of the day, he announced: 'I'm not going to eat a dead fish!'"

N.K. of South St. Paul: "My 3-year-old son said to me yesterday: 'Mom, guess what Dad and I are doing tomorrow!'

"I said: 'What?'

"He said: 'We're going ice-fishing'—and without missing a beat, he said: 'I sure hope I catch a big piece of ice.'"

BULLETIN BOARD MUSES: And when he got home, you just couldn't get him to stop talking about the huge chunk that got away.

Mrs. Soup of Oakdale: "Last Saturday, our 12-year-old went ice skating for the first time in years. He's not skated for . . . I don't know, probably since he was 5 or 6.

"The next day at church, during a free moment, I leaned over and asked him: 'Say, how was skating yesterday?'

"He looked at me, and he said: 'Good! Wasn't too bad.'

"I said: 'How'd you do?'

"And he said: 'Good! Would've been better if it hadn't been so icy.'"

Beth of White Bear Lake: "We were at Pizza Hut the other night, and we had kind of a long wait with our four kids.

"My 8-year-old was lookin' around, and he saw the menus sitting there. He started reading it, and he asked: 'Mom, what's a soft drink?'

"I said: 'Well, Christopher, what do *you* think a soft drink is?'

"And he said: 'One without ice?'"

A.C. of St. Paul: "About two years ago, I was baby-sitting for a little girl named Kelly. One night before bed, she asked for a glass of water with an ice cube in it. She started sucking on the ice, then shivered and said: 'When I'm a mommy, I'm gonna put the ice in the *refrigerator*—so it's not so cold.'"

Bob of Rochester: "My daughter, Carrie, works at a Montessori school with little kids.

"She was cleaning out the fridge, just dumping stuff into the sink and the trash. And one of the things was a baggie full of water.

"She looks down and sees this sad little girl with tears in her eyes. She asked what was the matter, and the little girl replies: 'You threw out my icicle.'"

Julie the Car Pool Mom: "My son goes to preschool. At the end of each preschool day, the teacher gives the students a message for the day. The message for yesterday was to please be very careful when you're going outside and to walk closely with your carpool parent or your mom and to be sure to watch out for cars.

"She said to the students, after she gave them the message: 'Do you know why I say that?'

"And one little voice piped up: 'It's because you love us?'

"And the teacher said: 'Yes.'

"I thought it was a sweet story."

Frozen Frieda of Crystal: "Little Misty came home from school, and her mother said: 'What did you learn in school today?'

"She said: 'We learned about Roger Luther King.'

"And her mother said: 'What did you learn about Roger Luther King?'

"And she said: 'He made a speech, and now white people can ride the bus.'"

Marsh Wiggle of White Bear Lake: "Frozen Frieda's story about 'Roger Luther King' jogged my memory from when my daughter was a precious and precocious 4-year-old.

"She came home from preschool on Martin Luther King Day very excited about what she had learned. She spoke fast because she was so excited: 'A long, long—really long—time ago, black people were treated mean. I mean, they weren't allowed to go the same places white people were, and they had to ride in the back of buses. Then'—she smiled, and her voice escalated a little—'Martin Luther, the king, came along and changed all that.'

"My daughter is Korean-born, and she paused and looked down at her arm and asked, seriously: '*My* skin is kind of brownie. Where would I have sat on the buses?'

"She made me cry.

"In first grade, she read a book about Martin Luther King Jr. and made a report about Rosa Parks. Now she knows it wasn't so very long ago.

"Thanks for reminding me."

Beth of White Bear Lake: "I have three kids in school, and last weekend they were all talking about how they had studied Martin Luther King.

"The kindergartner was telling me that black people had to sit in the back of the bus, way back when. I said: 'Well, why do you think that happened?' She said: 'I don't know.'

"So I asked my first-grader: 'Why do you think black people had to sit in the back of the bus?' She had no idea, either.

"So I asked Christopher, who's in third grade: 'Christopher, why do you think black people had to sit in the back of the bus?'

"He said: 'Well, I think back then, some white people were real buttheads.'

"Out of the mouths of babes, huh?"

A West Side Mom: "My son is often cold and asks me to hold him. I am busy, often, and tell him to go get his bathrobe when he's cold.

"This morning, he comes up to me and says: 'Mama, I'm cold.'

"I say: 'I'm not a bathrobe. Go get it.'

"He says: 'Mom, I don't want to use you for a bathrobe. I just want to use you for a mom.'

"How could I help but hold him then?"

Grandma Jeannette of St. Paul: "My co-worker is a busy mom with three little boys—ages 6, 2 and 1.

"Her 6-year-old son, Patrick, was feeling neglected one day, so he brought his mom the time-out timer and asked for seven minutes alone with her.

"Love how the little ones think."

Sunny Delight of Shoreview: "I recently had a birthday, and my sweet darling daughter gave me little Love Coupons for my birthday present.

"The first coupon said: 'Good for Hugs and Kisses.'

"And the second coupon said: 'Good for Kisses. (No Hugs Included.)'"

Grandma Karen of St. Paul: "I gave my 6-year-old grandson, Cory, a big kiss on the cheek. He took his hand and acted like he'd wiped it off.

"When I asked him if he wiped off my kiss, he said: 'No, Grandma. I just moved it a little.'"

Karen of Shoreview: "After putting my 7-year-old daughter, Jennifer, to bed one evening, my husband came out of her room chuckling to himself.

"He told me he had kissed Jennifer on her cheek. She rubbed her cheek with her hand. He asked her why she wiped off his kiss, and she said: 'Oh, no, Daddy. I'm only wiping off the spit. I'm keeping the kiss.'

"She comes up with things like that all the time. We sure do love her."

Mary Kay of Arden Hills: "When my 6-year-old son, Matt, was about 3, he would often spend up to 20 minutes sitting on the potty while reading his Disney picture books.

"One day, the circulation in his legs must have been a bit impaired from sitting too long. His legs must have fallen asleep.

"When he stood up, he looked down at the naked lower half of his chubby toddler body. With a look of total awe and excitement, he exclaimed: 'Mama! My legs are sparkling!'

"I can't help but chuckle when I think of the discoveries his body has awaiting him, when he is much, much older."

Toby's Mom of Mankato: "I am making pancakes for my soon-to-be-3-year-old. He is sitting there eating his pancakes shaped like Mickey Mouse; he's sitting on his leg, and all of a sudden he turns around to me, and he kinda looks down at his feet, and he says: 'Mom! My toes are buzzing! Want to come and hear 'em?'

"I thought that was a precious, precious thing to say."

The Home Creator of St. Paul: "My son Jack is 3, and today he came up to me and said: 'Mom, if you put your hand over your ear, you can hear the ocean!'

"I said: 'Yeah?'

"And he said: 'Try it!'

"So I put my hand over my ear, and I said: 'Yeah!'

"He said: 'I hear the ocean, and I hear people whispering! I hear people whispering . . . from New York! Wanna hear my ocean?' So he put his head up against my ear—ear to ear—so I could hear his ocean.

"And then he says: 'Mom, that's incredible! The ocean is supposed to be in the ocean—and instead, the ocean is in our ears!' "

Anonymous woman: "I have a 4-year-old daughter and a 5-year-old son. My daughter was telling me something which she didn't want my son to hear, so she was whispering it in my ear—and my son put his ear up to my other ear to see if he could hear what she was saying."

Steve of Hudson, Wis.: "I was driving along with my son the other day, and he was asking me questions about a personal conversation I'd had with a friend the day before.

"I looked at him and said: 'How come you ask me so many questions?'

"He looked at me, and he said: 'Well, you know, I've only been around seven years, Dad.'

"I felt kinda stupid."

Bill of Mahtomedi: "Seeing all of the coverage of the 25th anniversary of the moon walk brought back a memory of my son Eric, who's now about 25.

"Eric was just a little kid, barely able to walk himself, but he had perfected this graceful imitation of astronauts on the moon. He would walk around the living room, kind of in slow motion, as if there was a real light gravitational field that he was in. It was . . . charming.

"What a wonderful memory to come out of the past."

Ms. Boo of St. Paul: "Sometimes, being a single mother is really hard. You spend a lot of time worrying about whether you can pay the bills, and whether you can keep your kids in clothes. And you forget about the special little times. One happened to me in March.

"I was rocking my daughter to sleep by the light of the night light, and suddenly she sat up and looked me in the eyes and sang 'When You Wish Upon a Star' to me. And tears came to our eyes, and I darn near started bawling. I just hugged her and told her how proud I was of her."

Care Bear of Lake St. Croix Beach: "I have a 4-year-old boy whose name is Chance. He's a normal, spirited 4-year-old, but sometimes he'll say things that make you think: 'Where are you coming from?'

"Like the time he was at preschool screening and the instructor held up a colored card and asked him: 'What color is this, Chance?' And he said: 'Why? Don't *you* know?'

"But the story I really wanted to tell is about when his dad left for work one Sunday afternoon. My husband, Doug, drives a semi over the road, so he's gone all week until late Friday night. Well, Doug was saying how much he misses the kids and for them to be good, and Chance put his little hands on either side of his dad's face and said: 'Don't worry, Daddy. You just think of me, and I'll always be with you.'

"Wow, what a great kid."

Grandma Oh of Chisago City: "Jimmy, our 5-year-old grandson, informed his mom—Kim, our daughter—that he invited the little boy across the street to come and live with them.

"Kim asked why on earth he did that.

"Jimmy's response was: 'Well, both his mom and dad smoke, and they'll be dead soon, and he'll need a place to live.'

"Kim told him he shouldn't tell his friend that, because his friend would get scared.

" 'Oh, he didn't seem to mind!' Jimmy said."

Claire of South St. Paul, the youngest-ever Bulletin Board caller who spoke her mind understandably without the sound of an adult continually prompting her: "This is Claire. I hate how people get meaner and meaner and they throw cigarettes on the ground, and they always smoke and throw some more on the ground. We found two big puddles of . . . I mean, cigarettes, and they're so gross! I guess that's just all that I have to say. I'm 4 years old. Thank you. I love you. Bye-bye"—at which point Claire's mom can be heard in the background, for the first time, laughing and saying: "You don't say *that*!"

Arlene of the East Side: "One day last week, my 4-year-old's preschool class was going on a field trip to the Science Museum. All the parents and children were waiting in the hallway for the teacher to arrive—when out of the blue, my daughter, Alicia, announces to everyone: 'My mommy has chicken breasts!' "

Chris of White Bear Lake: "Well, it's Christmastime again—and what is a parent of a young child to do (besides buy stock in Toys 'R' Us)? Well, have the lovable portrait sitting, of course.

"My 3-year-old was the 'sitter,' if you will, and being 3, he felt obligated to ham it up a little—just 'cause . . . he's 3, I guess.

"The camera operator was trying her hardest to get a genuine smile out of him, and proceeded to reel off phrases like 'Your daddy has stinky feet!' and 'Fuzzy pickle!'

"Fuzzy pickle? What is that?

"Anyway, it worked. The sitting went fine, and it was over. We proceeded to exit the studio, and I began dressing him for the cold. The lobby was filled with eager, photogenic customers. As I began to put my son's coat on, he yelled: 'Daddy has stinky feet!'

"All eyes were on me, of course, and there was nothing left to do but turn tomato-red and leave."

BULLETIN BOARD NOTES: Any number of Bulletin Boarders called to observe that it could've been much, much worse. The little boy might have yelled: "Daddy has a fuzzy pickle!"

Jeri of Shell Lake, Wis.: "We have three daughters, and in September of 1990, the youngest one, who had just turned 2, wandered into the sun room of our home with a horrified look on her face—and looked as if she was about to spit something from her mouth.

"I grabbed a napkin, held it under her mouth—and as she spit, I realized that it smelled exactly like dog feces, which is what it turned out to be. I rinsed out her mouth, called the vet, found out our dog was healthy and refrained from kissing her for an hour and a half.

"But that's not the best part. The following May, when our second-grader was receiving First Communion, our priest was walking through the church, talking to the parents and asking anyone in the family if they had anything they'd like to pray about. Our 5-year-old—then 4—leaned forward to the priest and said, loudly enough for his portable microphone to broadcast it over the entire audience: 'One time, Kelsey ate a dog turd.' It brought down the house."

Pam of Apple Valley: "I have two sons, ages 8 and 4, and they were discussing Adam and Eve.

"The 8-year-old asked: 'How did Adam and Eve die?'

"And the 4-year-old said: 'They ate bad fruit.'"

Mrs. Soup of Oakdale: "My 7-year-old girl child came out of Sunday school, and she said: 'Mom, we celebrated Jesus' birthday today.'

"And I said: 'Well, that's neat. What'd you do?'

"And she said: 'We played a game.'

"I said: 'Oh! What kind of game?'

"She said: 'We played Pin the Tail on Mary!'

"And I was just about hysterical, and then the 12-year-old boy child said: 'You ... did ... not! You played Pin Mary on the Donkey.'

"Either way, I said I thought it sounded like it hurt."

Tammy of St. Paul: "I was talking to my sister on the telephone tonight, and she said that her husband and their daughter, who is 8, had gone to a church revival meeting, and they were sitting in the church when the 8-year-old said: 'Daddy, my chin really hurts. I think you should take me home.'

"And my brother-in-law said: 'Oh, it's just about over. Just hang in there a little while, and we'll go home.'

"And a few minutes later, she said: 'Daddy, my head really hurts. I think you should take me home.'

"And he said: 'Do your chin and your head *really* hurt?'

"And she said: 'Well, my chin really does—but I had to hit myself in the head to make *that* hurt.'"

Jeanne of St. Paul: "Our son attended a private, parochial school. The pastor was a very strict man.

"One day, when Steven was in third grade, he came home very excited: 'Mom! Mom! Monsignor talked to me!'

"I had to calm him down.

"Finally I said: 'What did Monsignor say?'

"'Zip up, young man!'"

Auntie of West St. Paul: "Our parish priest was making a visit to my nephew's home.

"Knocked on the door, and the little 4-year-old boy went to the door and saw the priest.

"He called to his dad: 'Hey, Dad! That guy that works for God is here!'"

Lisa of St. Paul: "My 5-year-old son, Tyler, started kindergarten this year at a Catholic school, and he came home from school on the first day with a bottle of holy water. I asked him who'd given it to him, and he said: 'I don't know, Mom. Just some kid's father—but he wouldn't let us drink it.'

"I laughed and asked him if it was Father Jack. He looked at me like I was crazy and said: 'Mom, there's no Jack in our class.'

"Made me realize I need to go visit church more often—and bring him along."

Lori of Woodbury: "Yesterday, Sunday, there was a commotion when my family came home from church. I usually attend church sitting at the kitchen table here with the Sunday paper. So I asked: 'What's going on?'

"My husband said that on the way home from church, Lindsay, my 10-year-old, pulled out a blessed Host—you know, the body of Christ—from her pocket. My husband told her to place it in her mouth right away, and proceeded to scold her and explain that this is sacred and should never be taken out of church. And he asked her what in the world would ever make her do such a thing.

"She said: 'I just wanted to bring it home for Mom, because I worry about her not ever going to communion.'

"I thought that was the sweetest thing—and made me feel so guilty that [Bulletin Board notes: We detected a big sigh here] maybe I better think about going to church again."

Terri of Cottage Grove: "My 2½-year-old niece, Kelli, went with her neighbor girl to church for First Communion practice. The pastor has the children cup their hands, and when he gives them the Host—in this case, a piece of bread—he says: 'God be with you.'

"Apparently this made quite an impression on my niece. She came home and told her mother to cup her hands and bend down. Kelli took a piece of bread from her sandwich, placed it in her mother's hands, and whispered, in her most angelic voice: 'God will get you.'"

Kimberly of Cottage Grove: "Recently, I decided to start going back to church, and I was explaining to my 3-year-old son that we had to go there and be quiet.

"He asked me why we were going. I said we were going to learn about God.

"He looked me right in the eye, straight-faced, and asked me if we were going to be learning about 'damn it,' too.

"Guess he got that from my husband."

Mark of White Bear: "I was goin' out with a girl back in the '70s, and she had a boy named Clint, and we were eatin' at my parents' house, and Clint started sayin' the F word at the table.

"Lynn was really embarrassed, and after my mom looked at me and said 'I know where he got *that* from,' Lynn tried to do some damage control and said: 'No, that's how he says "frog." Say "frog," Clint. Say "frog." '

"And Clint said: 'Frog. F—in' frog.' "

Julie of Hastings: "My sister and I were watching a movie with her 5-year-old little girl. It was a rated-G movie, but it had the word a— in it. The sentence was: 'That guy's a dumb a—.'

"My niece looked over to my sister and said: 'Mommy, that little boy said a bad word!'

"And her mom goes: 'I know. We shouldn't use that word.'

"And my niece goes: 'Daddy told me *never* to use the word 'dumb.'

"I thought that was adorable."

Barb of Vadnais Heights: "I took my little nephew, 3 years old, to *Snow White and the Seven Dwarfs* along with my son, who is 5. Halfway through the movie, when they were going through the dwarfs' names, my little nephew said: 'Auntie, why are they calling that little dwarf Bastard?'

"I just had to put my hands over my mouth, I was laughing so hard. I had to tell my little nephew: 'Honey, they're calling him Bashful.'

"He doesn't understand what bashful is, but he knows it's a lot better than being called Bastard.

"Oh, and by the way: I'm sure he got that word off TV."

Elaine of Mendota Heights: "My daughter was 3 at the time, and my mother had been baby-sitting with her one evening, and they watched *Back to the Future*. And, in one part of the movie, they use 'son of a bitch.'

"The next day, my mother and I took my daughter to the Apple Valley zoo, and we went into the bat exhibit. It was very dark in there, and as we were standing there, she said: 'Son of a bitch it's dark in here.'

"And, of course, we had to emerge out into the light, with all these people looking at us."

C.J.B. of St. Paul: "On Saturday, my niece—who's 5 years old—was in a bike accident. Her mom had to take her to the emergency room.

"Bobbie Jo hates it when people swear, and she calls every naughty word 'the B word.' Shortly after getting a shot from the doctor for pain, she looked up at her mom and said: 'Oh, please, Mommy, just once I wish I could say the B word. Just *once*.'"

The Transplanted St. Paulite of Roseville: "My almost-2-year-old daughter went out shopping with my husband last Friday night. She came back home, and I asked her: 'Did you get to see Santa Claus?'

" 'Yeah.'

" 'Did you sit on his lap?'

" 'Yeah.'

" 'Did he ask you what you wanted for Christmas?'

" 'Yeah.'

" 'What did you say?'

" 'Please.'"

Jim of Woodbury: "Today I was fixing my daughter's hair, and my son, who is 5, was running around.

"I said: 'Matthew, settle down.'

"And he said: 'I might consider it if you'd say the word "Please."'

"I said: 'OK, Matthew. Please settle down.'

"And he said: 'Dad, that wasn't very difficult, was it?'"

Dory of Wyoming: "I was handing out candy on Halloween, and this little girl about 2 years old came to my door. She had a little bunny outfit on.

"I went to the door with the candy, and her mom said: 'Say "Trick or treat!"' So she says 'Trick or treat!' and I give her the candy, and she starts walking away, and her mom says: 'Say "Thank you!"'

"And she turns around and blows me a kiss. I just thought that was *so* cute."

Bob Woolley of St. Paul, after Halloween: "One little girl looked to be about 3 years old. She was wearing an adorable tiger costume. She held out her bag when I opened the door, but didn't say anything.

"Her dad was standing next to her and prompted her, in a loud whisper: 'What do you *say?*' No answer. 'What do you *say?*'

"Finally, she looked at me with big, pleading eyes and said: 'Pleeeeease?'"

A Grandma of Vadnais Heights: "My husband went to the door to find two young ladies standing there—without costume.

"He said to them: 'This is Halloween. You're supposed to be ghosts or goblins. You're not very scary.'

"And the little girl said: 'We're teenagers. Isn't that scary enough?'"

L.H. of St. Paul, on Halloween: "When Luke, who's now 16, was just a little guy—from about 2 to 5—he would sit out in our pumpkin patch the day before Halloween and wait for the Great Pumpkin to arrive.

"This year, we went out and picked out pumpkins for everybody, and his brother picked out this huge, giant pumpkin for him. Luke came home from work, and he got so excited about this pumpkin. He had to weigh it; it weighed 67 pounds.

"Then he carves out the pumpkin so it'll fit on his head, calls us into the kitchen—and his dad says: 'Hey, Luke, the Great Pumpkin's finally arrived.'

"And now there he is, all of 16 years old, outside handing out candy to the kids, so excited. The doorbell'll ring, and here he is, runnin' around the house, goin' 'Where's my head? Where's my head?'

"You're never too old for Halloween."

Merle of Wisconsin: "Today I was gathering up the squash in the garden, and my 4-year-old son was helping me. We were taking the pumpkins and squash and putting them in his wagon, and then he realized that another opportunity existed, and that was to take the big, pale, bloated cucumbers that are rotten and put them on the road and ride his tricycle over them—and they would squash in a really satisfying way.

"So he did this a few times, and when he came back into the patch to get some more, he was very excited about it. I saw him stop and look around—and it dawned on him that he would be able to do this *all day* if he wanted to, because there were so many big, rotten cucumbers that we just didn't get to.

"He stood there for a minute, and then he sighed and he said: 'Oh, I'm *rich*.'"

Theresa Lippert of St. Paul: "Several years ago, we moved into a nice house in St. Paul. It's not too fancy, but it is big, and my 7-year-old son, Jesse, was giving a neighborhood boy a tour. My husband overheard the little boy say to Jesse: 'Are you guys rich?'

"And Jesse replied: 'No, but we lead a happy life.' That was for us a perfect moment in parenthood."

Daddy the Omnipotent of West St. Paul: "A few weeks ago when I came home from work, I realized just how much faith my 20-month-old daughter, Hannah, has in me.

"It was a very rainy night, and I was greeted with the usual 'Daddy, play outside. Hannah swing?' As I tried to explain to her that we couldn't play outside because we'd get wet, she just kept repeating 'Outside. Swing?' Finally I just said: 'Hannah, we can't play outside because it is raining.'

"She looked at me totally unfazed and said: 'Daddy, fix rain'—and headed for the door."

Jan of Northfield: "Earlier tonight, I was sitting with my family, having dinner. My daughter is not yet 5, and she's really working on learning a lot of words—and she doesn't really understand a lot of what she's talking about.

"She turned to me, and she said: 'You know, Daddy's a genius.'

"And being a proud wife, I said: 'Yes, honey, I know.'

"And she looked at me—waitin' for, like, a reaction. Maybe she'd said a bad word?

"And I said: 'Do you know what that means?'

"She said: 'No.'

"I said: 'That means Daddy's really, really smart.'

"And she said: 'Uh-oh! Wrong word!'"

Mom of White Bear Lake: "My almost-3-year-old was going to the bathroom, and she kept telling her grandma: 'I'm a girl, Grandma. I'm a girl. And my brother is a boy.'

"Finally, Grandma was saying to her: 'Well, what do you mean?'

"And she said: 'He's a boy because he has a pee-pee.'

"Grandma said: 'Well, what do girls have?'

"And she said: 'Girls have brains.'

"Wow! Don't they learn young?"

Grandma of Cottage Grove: "Recently, I had my 3- and 4-year-old granddaughters over for the night. Early in the morning, they come running into my bedroom and climbed up into bed with me and snuggled up close.

"The 3-year-old said: 'Grandma, I'm a girl, and you're a girl, and Sammy Jo's a girl—right?'

"And I said: 'That's right, Rachael.'

"And she said: 'And poor Grandpa! He is just a man.'

"And I thought: 'My daughter's sure raisin' *that* kid right.'"

Tom of Lino Lakes: "While attending a family reunion in a county park one summer, my 4-year-old daughter had to use the restroom—and, of course, the only restrooms in the park were the outdoor, two-holer types.

"Grandma thought she'd be helpful and take her to the bathroom—and on the way, she forewarned her that when she stepped into the outhouse, it would probably have an odor.

"My daughter said: 'That shouldn't be any problem. I have to use the same bathrooms as my dad at home.'"

Mike's Wife of Shoreview: "My husband taught our 3-year-old that if she pulled his finger, he would [expel a posterior breeze]. One day, when he was real busy around the house, she walked up to him and pulled his finger. And he hadn't noticed.

"She gets a big question mark over her head and says: 'Hmmmmm. Empty'—and walks away."

BULLETIN BOARD WONDERS: Are we to take it that on every other occasion, Mike delivered as promised?

J.M. of Clear Lake, Wis.: "I have this little cousin who was 2½ at the time, and he was at a basketball game, and we have this cheer that goes: 'Hey, all you Warrior fans! Stand up and clap your hands!'

"My cousin interpreted it a little differently. He stood up and proudly said: 'Hey, all you Warrior fans, stand up and crap your pants.' You can just see him looking around at everybody—wondering, you know, if that's what everybody was doing."

Mr. Sentimental of Hudson, Wis.: "When our daughter was about 2½, I was given a pair of excellent tickets to the Minnesota Gophers vs. Fighting Illini men's basketball game on very short notice. My wife had a meeting that night, and it was too late to even think about finding a babysitter. I decided that while my daughter wouldn't understand the game, she'd get a kick out of the colorful and noisy crowd at Williams Arena and would probably be entertained by the running and jumping of the great big guys on the court.

"We had a great time, but my daughter seemed unduly quiet on the way back to the car, and I thought she might be experiencing some sort of sensory overload from the game. Finally, as I was strapping her into her car seat, she asked, 'Daddy, when you go to the hospital to have a baby, do you have to take your underpants off so the baby can come out?'

"So much for my ability to read even little minds."

Kris of Burnsville: "I work at a day-care center in Eagan. We were sittin' around yesterday, and a little girl said to me: 'My mom told me that *she* wears my dad's pants in *this* family.'"

Owen's Mom of St. Paul: "The other night, my 6-year-old son, Owen, was arguing with his 6-year-old friend Russell. My husband finally asked them what they were arguing about, and my son's response was: 'We're practicing for when we argue with our wives.'"

Mary of Maplewood: "Last night, we were watching *Old Yeller* with our kids. At the end, I was explaining how the boy, Travis, had to be the man around the house while his dad was gone for so long. And Mikey, who's 6 years old, turned to me and said: 'I wish Daddy would go away for a long time—like a month or so.'

"I said: 'Oh, Mikey, wouldn't you miss your dad if he was gone that long?'

"And he says: 'No—'cause then I could be in charge. Me and you could argue, and I could be lazy all the time, and you could do all the cookin'.'

"My husband and I looked at each other and just burst out laughing. I thought: That really said it all. That was quite a mouthful."

BULLETIN BOARD REPLIES: If you can laugh, Mary, so can we.

Mary of Como Park: "A few years ago, my daughter was 4 and she was heavily into Barbie dolls. She received her first Ken doll: Hawaiian Fun Ken. She was playing with him, and her older brother and I were doing something nearby, and she decided to change Ken's pants.

"She took off Ken's swimsuit, and in a 4-year-old *horrified* voice, she goes: 'Oh, my gosh! Ken has no private parts!'

"Her brother, who was five years older, says to her: 'Well, I guess we better change his name to Hawaiian No-more-fun Ken.'"

Missy of Mahtomedi: "My daughter was playing with her Barbie dolls this morning. She was sitting on the floor, and she had Barbie and a prince, and she was pretending like they were getting married. And she said: 'Barbie, do you take this prince to be your awfully wedded husband?'

"Ain't it the truth?"

BULLETIN BOARD REPLIES: Not necessarily.

Svenska of White Bear Lake: "Years ago, my two little girls— 2 and 3 years old—decided to play house one day.

"One said: 'Hello! My name is Mrs. Ollie Peterson.'

"The other girl said: 'Oh! *My* name is Mrs. Ollie Peterson.'

"The first daughter hesitated, and then smiled brightly and said: 'Oh! I guess we have the same husband!'"

BULLETIN BOARD MUSES: Sounds to us like a TV movie.
Starring Jaclyn Smith as Mrs. Ollie Peterson.
Also starring Connie Sellecca as Mrs. Ollie Peterson.
With Robert Urich as Ollie Peterson, Lisa Hartman Black as Ollie Peterson's long-suffering mistress, and Jerry Orbach as the attorney for one (if not both) of "The Two Mrs. Ollie Petersons."

Jeannette of North Branch: "When I was a new stepmom, my second-grader came home from school and announced: 'Mom, Jenny told me she French-kissed a kid at school.'

"Well, I hadn't imagined that kids their ages would even know what French kissing was, so I dubiously said to my kindergarten-age Jenny: 'Jennifer, Carmen says that you French-kissed a boy at school today.'

"Her indignant response was: 'I did *not*! It was a *girl*.'"

Shelly of Champlin: "My sister and my niece—her name's Casey; she's 6 years old—were visiting Grandpa, and they were sitting at the table talking about how a family member is getting a divorce. Casey was taking it all in, and Grandpa said: 'You'll never get a divorce, will you, Casey?'

"And she said: 'No—'cause *I'm* gonna marry a girl!'"

Single Mother of St. Paul: "My son Sean was about 5, and my daughter Erin was about 3½. We were waiting for the bus at the bus stop, and my daughter says: 'Mom, when I grow up, I'm gonna marry you.'

"And my son said: 'Erin, don't be silly. Girls can't get married. I'm gonna marry you, aren't I, Mom?'"

Bob of Rochester: "The 3- and 4-year-olds were sitting and having lunch together, and my daughter Coleen overheard the little boys talking.

"One little boy was shaking his head and saying, with a cute little lisp: 'I jutht don't think I can make that dethithion. I jutht don't think I can make that dethithion.'

"Coleen was curious, so she asked him what was the matter. He said: 'I jutht can't make the dethithion who I'm gonna marry.'

"She assured him that he wouldn't have to make that decision until he was an adult. He heaved a sigh of relief and said: 'Oh, you know, you're right, Coleen. I've thtill got a few yearth.'

"Love those kids."

Theresa of St. Paul: "Danny, who's going to be 6 in June, was having his breakfast this morning, and by mistake I gave him a regular-size glass and a regular-size spoon. He pointed out to me that he needed his small, yellow glass and his little spoon, and I said: 'Well, Danny, when you turn 6, you're gonna have a regular glass and a regular spoon.'

"He said: 'I know, Mom. Then I'll be bigger, and you can give my spoon and my glass away.'

"I said: 'Well, I think I'll keep them for my grandchildren.'

"And he looked at me, very seriously, and said: 'I didn't know you had any grandchildren.'

"And I said: 'Well, I don't right now, but when you or Sam or Jesse grow up and get married and have children, then I'll have grandchildren.'

"He looked at me and said: 'I'll miss you, Mom.'

"And I said: 'When you get married?'

"And he said: 'No. I'm too shy to get married.'"

Jodell of parts undisclosed: "I was talking to my 6-year-old daughter, Caitlin, this morning and asked her why she wanted to grow up so fast. She's always wanting to be older.

"She said she wanted to be a teenager. I asked her why. She said: Because she could have a boyfriend.

"I said: 'Well, why do you want a boyfriend?' She said: 'Because then we could get married.'

"I said: 'Well, why do you want to be married?' *[Bulletin Board interjects: So she doesn't have to answer so many darned questions?]*

"She said: 'Because then I can have kids.'

"I said: 'Why do you want to have kids?'

"She said: 'So then I can be bossy.'

"I guess that's why I'm a parent, too."

Phil of Northfield: "A couple of years ago, my family was attending the rehearsal for my sister-in-law's wedding. My oldest, 5-year-old Aaron, was the ring bearer.

"During the rehearsal, as the bride and her father were making their way down the aisle, I held my 4-year-old daughter, Brianne, in my arms.

"Watching the father and his daughter make their way to the altar, I was foreseeing my future and realized how very much I loved my little girl.

"I held her tightly and whispered: 'Princess, do you know that in about 20 years, that will be you and me going down the aisle? I will be so sad, and I will cry all the way because that means my little girl is all grown up, and I will be losing my little Princess.'

"She looked me straight in the eye and smiled as she said: 'Don't worry, Daddy. You'll be a grandpa by then.'"

BULLETIN BOARD REPLIES: Her brother's child, with any luck—and his wife's, of course.

Oh, and one more thing: You won't be losing your Princess. You'll have your Princess 'til the day you—with any luck—die.

She'll be gaining—with any luck—her Prince.

Big difference.

Charly of St. Paul: "I work at a preschool, and we were going to have our pictures taken one day last week.

"Now, normally I don't wear a lot of makeup—and when I do, I usually get comments from my family like 'What's that on your face?' or 'What're ya wearin' makeup for?'

"On this particular day, I decided to put on a little blush and lipstick. My 10-year-old son came downstairs that morning, stared at me for a few minutes and said: 'Mom, I think you look very beautiful'—and gave me a big hug."

Donna of River Falls, Wis.—whose tone of voice suggested the deepest mutual affection (in case you get to wondering): "My son Curt—who is 5—and I have a bedtime ritual. After Curt gets settled in his bed, I read a book to him.

"Then I say: 'Good night.' Curt replies: 'Good night.'

"Then we hug, and I say: 'I love you.' And Curt says: 'I love you.'

"Then he gives me a little push and says: 'Now, get out of my room.'"

Deb of St. Louis Park: "One night, a friend and I were baby-sitting my 5-year-old sister, Katie, who refused to go to bed. We'd send her upstairs; five minutes later, she'd be back down with one excuse or another.

"Finally, I walked upstairs with her, put her in bed and went downstairs with a warning to stay in bed. I told her good night with a note of finality—as in 'This is the end of it!'

"She got mad at me, and when I got to the bottom of the steps, I heard her getting out of bed. I turned around, and she was at the top of the steps, with her hands on her hips.

"And she said, 'Well! You can just kiss my butt good night!'

"I turned around so she wouldn't see me laugh."

Kathy of Como: "My 2½-year-old son, Tony, was crying in the middle of the night. I ran to his room to see what was the matter. He was half asleep, crying that he wanted a hamburger.

"I calmed him down by telling him that I would go and make him one as soon as he would lay his head back down on the pillow. He did, and as soon as I thought he was asleep, I crept out of his room.

"I got to the top of the stairs when he yelled in his loudest voice: 'With *pickles!*' "

Julie of River Falls, Wis., speaking of her 4-year-old son: "I was putting him to bed, and I had just gotten done reading him a story—and, oh, I got a stomachache, so I just went out for a second, and I came back and I thought he was asleep.

"I said: 'Alex, are you sleeping?'

"He had his eyes closed and a real goofy look on his face. He goes: 'Mom, quit buggin' me! I'm watchin' Baloo the Bear on my eye TV.'

"All I could do was chuckle and laugh and just kiss him goodnight. What else can you do?"

BULLETIN BOARD REPLIES: Well, you could sit down and watch with him.

Crystal of Newport: "I'm baby-sitting right now? And this little girl named Shannon? She was telling me about her little gymnastics class, and she goes: 'Guess what! This little girl can do a Mermaid off the end of the balance beam!'

"And I go: 'A what?'

"And she goes: 'A Mermaid!'

"And I go . . . I go: 'What?'

"And she goes: 'An Ariel!'

"And I go: 'Ohhhh!' I thought that was so cute, because she thinks an aerial is a Mermaid."

Deb of Shoreview: "I was reminded of this a few days ago when I was watching a Disney cartoon with my 7-year-old.

"When he was about 4, he was learning about the planets in preschool. I asked him to name some planets for me. He said: 'The Earth, and Mars, and Saturn, and Goofy.'

"I guess it makes perfect sense when you're 4."

BULLETIN BOARD REPLIES: Actually, Deb, it makes perfect sense when you're much, much older than 4.

The boy was trying to remember Pluto! And it came out Goofy.

We've gotten them confused, momentarily, ourselves.

Linnea's Mom of Mounds View: "I was just fixing my daughter her lunch while she was watching *The Lion King* and offered her the choice of a tuna or salami sandwich. She said that she'd have a Tuna Matata sandwich for lunch.

"Good one, huh?"

Julie of Maplewood: "My youngest daughter, Katie, who just turned 3 in July, loves to sing—especially when she sits on the potty ... which she does often, since we're trying to potty-train her.

"Recently, after a day at the beach, I put her on the potty at the public restroom there, and as I stood outside the stall waiting for her, I heard her singing that song from *The Lion King* movie, 'Hakuna Matata.'

"She sang 'Hakuna Matata, Hakuna Matata, Hakuna Matata'— and then, in the same tune and without missing a beat, she sang: 'I peed in the potty.' "

Leslie of parts undisclosed: "My cousin's son, John, graduated from high school this past spring, but I will always remember the open house I hosted when he was about 4 at which he announced to the assembled guests that he was going 'potty.'

"He was gone only a few seconds before he returned, his eyes as large as saucers, and he exclaimed in a very incredulous voice: 'Who went *blue*?' "

Benjamin and Rebeccah's Mom of the Midway: "I'm a day-care provider. One morning when my daughter woke up, I had a houseful of kids, so I pulled off her cloth diaper, dropped it in the upstairs toilet for a rinse and left it there for a while.

"When I went back to toss it in the diaper pail a few hours later, there was a mouse sitting on top of the diaper—in the toilet, looking at me. I screamed, slammed the toilet lid closed, closed the bathroom door and called my husband at work and told him to come home and remove that mouse.

"In the meantime, our 4-year-old wanted to know why I'd screamed. I told him about the mouse, but warned him not to tell the day-care kids. I didn't want to scare them.

"He promised not to tell, but I could tell he was having a hard time keeping his promise when I heard him singing 'Mouse in the toilet' to the tune of 'Waltzing Matilda.'"

Barbie of Hugo: "My second-grade son just got a buzz haircut. The other night, as I was putting him to bed, I was running my fingers over his head.

"He said: 'What are you doin', Mom?'

"And I said: 'Oh, I'm just feeling your haircut. It feels like mouse fur.'

"His eyes lit up, and he rolled over and said: 'I know where a dead one is. You wanna go feel it?'"

Patty Mack of St. Paul: "This is a story I heard from a parent the other day. She's a single mom who lives with her daughter, Caitlan, who is 7 years old. It was nighttime, and Caitlan heard an ambulance go by and got scared. So she asked her mom if she could hop in bed with her. And so she did.

"Then she said: 'Can I go get Toby?'—which is her stuffed Toucan. She sleeps with a bird. Anyway, her mom says 'Sure,' so she goes, gets Toby, brings it back into bed and says: 'Toby's scared, too.'

"When her mom asked why, she said, 'Because I just told Toby about duck hunting.'"

Bonnie Out East: "My son's girlfriend told me that her 3½-year-old nephew, Nick, was afraid of the fireworks his relatives were setting off, so his mom brought him to their porch to sit with his great-grandpa.

"Still fearful, little Nick said to the old man: 'How 'bout if we go inside and watch the news.'"

BULLETIN BOARD MUSES: And then the old man can get scared.

Uncle Mark of St. Paul: "My niece is a very willful little child. She was playing hide-and-seek the other day with her friends in the neighborhood. All the other children wanted to quit playing hide-and-seek and begin playing Simon Says—upon which my niece threw a great fit on the ground.

"Well, after a lot of crying and whining and fighting, she agreed to play Simon Says if she'd get to be Simon. So she gets all the kids lined up, and she says: 'Simon says: Hide.'"

Grandma Kay of Roseville: "He was 3½ years old, and I was reading him a bedtime story.

"It's a warm, summer evening. The windows are open. A little breeze.

"All of a sudden, there's a noise in the other room. He looks at me with his big eyes, and he says: 'Grandma, you go check it out. I'll go hide.'

"This is my grandson. Smart, huh?"

Mighty M. of Eagan: "I'm calling with a cute kid story—and the cute kids weren't even mine! Amazing!

"I live in a security building. Last night about 9:30, we got a phone call, and somebody said: 'This is the Eagan police. We have a medical emergency. Could you let us in?'

"So I did—and then I got nervous and thought: 'I don't know who they are; I'd better go check this out.' So I did. My husband followed me, because he didn't think I should be doing this alone.

"We got down there, and sure enough, there was a cop car out front. The police asked if we'd let the ambulance drivers in when they got there. So we did that—and right on their heels, two darling little boys, about 7 or 8 years old, came racing in the door and said: 'What's *happening*? Why is that ambulance here?'

"I said: 'I have no idea. Somebody must have been hurt or must have gotten sick.'

"And one of the kids said: 'Yeah, they could have had a heart attack—or maybe be pregnant.'"

"And the other kid said: 'Yeah, or they could have constipation. That happened to me once.'

"We tried *really* hard not to laugh until they were gone."

Audrey of Eagan: "One weekend, our 6-year-old grandson, Cody, was staying overnight at our home. He got dressed shortly after we got up the next morning.

"When he came out into the kitchen, I noticed he had his sweater on inside-out, so I said: 'Oh, Cody, did you know that you put your sweater on inside-out?'

"And he said: 'Oh, it doesn't matter, Grandma. It's warm on both sides.'"

Jenny of Roseville: "A few years ago, we took our two sons, ages 3 and 4, to a nice restaurant. As the hostess was seating us, she asked if we needed booster chairs. The 4-year-old declined. When she returned with a bright-red booster, he changed his mind.

"Disappointment set in when she returned this time with a plain brown booster. Turning to his little brother, he tried a simple trade. No way.

"'But your favorite color is green,' said the 4-year-old, 'and if we trade, you can pretend the brown one is green!'"

Nowhere Man of St. Paul: "My son, who's less than 18 months old and who has a vocabulary of fewer words than his father has extremities, went with us to one of my favorite Chinese restaurants.

"He's been a very good boy in restaurants, but not yesterday. He wasn't unhappy; he was loud, squirmy, and finally decided to start screaming for the heck of it right as our food arrived.

"The couple at the next table obviously noticed; they were staring. So we decided: 'Well, let's do carry-out'—starting with carrying out my son to the car.

"So we pick him up. The first thing he does is stop screaming, turn to the couple at the next table, wave, and say 'Bye-bye.' I'm beginning to wonder if all that rambunctiousness was deliberate. He's a smart kid."

Kirsten of St. Paul: "My little 22-month-old niece was just being yelled at by her grandmother for . . . I don't even know what she did; she tried to climb up on the counter and grab a cookie . . . something along those lines.

"As my mom is yelling at her . . . not yelling, but telling her she shouldn't be doing what she was doing, she looks up with these big brown eyes, and she opens her arms, and . . . she doesn't have that many words, mind you; she only has 10 or 15, total . . . and she looks up at my mom with her arms wide open, and she says: 'Hug. Big hug.'

"And I thought: 'What a scammer!'"

A Mom of Inver Grove Heights: "My 8-year-old daughter, Amber, came home from school the other day to tell me that a Girl Scout recruiter had explained to her about how the Girl Scout system works—which is that she would first be a Daisy Girl, and then a Brownie, and then eventually she would become a Girl Scout.

"That night, we signed her up for Girl Scouts—and on the way home the next day, she said: 'I forget now, Mom. Am I gonna be a Girl Scout or a Cupcake?'"

Jane of Mahtomedi: "I bought a coconut the other day at the grocery store. My kids have never seen the inside of a real coconut, so I thought we'd do an experiment.

"I was telling my 7- and 4-year-olds that there was milk inside and we had to drain it before we cracked it open. And without missing a beat, my 7-year-old says: 'Is it 1 or 2 percent?'"

Kath of Woodbury: "My daughter was tellin' us about this report she's doin' for school. They all have to do a president.

"She's doing Abraham Lincoln, and somebody else is doing Grant, and somebody else is doing Fillmore, and somebody else is doing Kermit.

"I said: 'Kermit?' And I'm thinkin' and I'm thinkin', and I said: 'Oh, do you mean Garfield?'

"She said: 'Yeah, yeah! Garfield!'"

Connie of White Bear Lake: "My 4-year-old grandson, Paul, and his 2-year-old sister, Ingrid, do a lot of pretending. Paul is really into cowboy hats, boots, guns, etc.

"One day, Paul says to Ingrid: 'I'll be Matt Dillon, and you can be Kitty.'

"She says: 'OK!'—and promptly drops on all fours and starts meowing."

Julie of Centuria, Wis.: "I threw out some old cereal the other day for the birds, and my little girl saw me do it.

"Yesterday, I came into the living room, and here were Cheerios sprinkled all over the living-room floor. My 4-year-old, Jennifer, is standing there, and I asked her: 'What are you doing?'

"She said: 'I'm feeding the birds!'

"And there was my 1-year-old, Hannah, sitting on the floor, eating the cereal.

"Jennifer says: 'Hannah is my bird!' "

Daddy of the West End: "I was having some quiet time with my son this evening at his bedtime, and I said to him: 'You know, sweetheart, you're the apple of my eye.'

"And he said: 'Well, what does that mean, Daddy?'

"And I said: 'That means that you're the best thing in my life.'

"And he said: 'You know what, Daddy?'

"And I said: 'What?'

"And he said: 'You're the best thing in my apple. . . . Do we have any Apple Jacks?' "

Bonnie of Grantsburg, Wis.: "This morning, my son was eating breakfast, having his cereal, and he sneezed.

"I said: 'Bless you!'

"And he said: 'Look, Mommy! I blessed a Rice Krispie out!' "

Grandpa George of Mendota Heights: "At a family gathering on Mother's Day, our grandson, 3-year-old Andrew, gave a good, healthy sneeze—for which he covered his face—and then turned to his mother and said: 'I got bless-you on my hand, Mom.' "

T-Bird of parts undisclosed: "My 8-year-old boy, after his third day of 103-degree fever, is laying on the couch, and he says: 'Did you ever notice how when you're sick, if everybody in the world had a Butterfinger bar and you didn't have one, you wouldn't even care?' "

Pam of Oakdale: "My 4½-year-old son is having a bout with an ear infection, so he's on an antibiotic. Well, this antibiotic isn't agreeing with his system.

"Last night, he said: 'Mommy, my butt threw up.'"

Tired Mom of Eagan: "My 2½-year-old has been interested in helping me cook lately, so she sometimes associates food with other things.

"Today, after having a loose stool in the potty chair, she said: 'Mommy! Look! I made a pancake!'"

Doctor Friendly of St. Paul: "I just saw, in my office, a very cute, blond, 7-year-old girl for an ear infection. As I usually do with children her age, I let her choose the form of her antibiotic: 'Would you like the kind of pills you swallow whole, the kind of pills you can chew up, or liquid medicine?'

"She thought hard for a few seconds—and then, with *adorable* politeness, responded: 'None, thank you.'"

Bob of Outer Space: "The other day, we switched my 7-year-old daughter's antibiotic from liquid form to a chewable form, telling her that this was what the grown-ups did.

"She took one taste of it and said: 'Does this come in any other flavor except gross?'"

A Student Home for the Summer of Stillwater: "The other night, my parents went out, and I was home alone with my little sister. And thinking that since I'm only home for the summer, it would be nice to have a little special evening, I went and bought veggie burgers and tabbouleh and cucumbers with dip. *[Bulletin Board notes: That does sound like the epitome of—as you put it— "little special."]*

"My sister's 10. She took a bite of her veggie burger and said that she didn't like it. I said: 'Well, that's an acquired taste, Christina, and maybe in a couple weeks, you can try it again and you'll like it a little bit more.'

"Next, she tried the tabbouleh—and looked at me, and had the look that she didn't like it very much. I said: 'Well, Christina, I like tabbouleh—but I didn't like it before. Now, what does that make tabbouleh?'—thinking that she would say it was an acquired taste.

"She looked at me and said: 'That just makes it gross.'"

Chrissy of Inver Grove Heights: "On the Fourth of July, my 2½-year-old daughter, Samantha, and I were cutting vegetables for a holiday salad—and much to my surprise, she was eatin' the vegetables as fast as I could cut 'em. Keep in mind: A week ago, if a vegetable was ever found on her plate, the child would go into complete and total shock.

"I turned to her and asked, seriously: 'When did you start liking vegetables, Samantha?'

"And giving me the most serious face that she could, she looks at me and says: 'Oh, about 10 o'clock yesterday, Mom.'"

Peggy of Woodbury, with a story meant as a 16th-birthday gift to her daughter: "When Jenny was about half the age she is now, we were watching a Lassie movie. At one point, Lassie pals up with a soldier on a noisy battlefield. Of course, even with all of the bullets and bombs, she saves his life—but becomes shell-shocked and begins to act weird.

"Jenny asked what was wrong with Lassie, and as we tried to explain it, we used the phrase 'Her mind snapped.'

"'Oh!' she said. '*That's* what that noise was.'"

Barb of Mounds View: "When my 9-year-old was 4, he very much wanted our black Lab to have puppies—so he snuck a couple of eggs from the refrigerator and was caught burying them in the back yard. He explained that he wished our dog, April, would sit on the eggs and they would hatch into little puppies."

Denise of Woodbury: "I have a sister, whose name is Mary, who was driving down the street one day with my nephew Andrew in the back. And as they were driving along, Andrew was entertaining himself by reciting some nursery rhymes.

"He's going along, and he gets to 'Mary Had a Little Lamb.' He's going 'Mary had a little lamb, little lamb, little . . .'—and he pauses. Dead still. Looks up to the front seat and says: 'Do you have a *lamb?*'"

Leah of Minneapolis: "A woman I used to work with kept the office entertained with frequent stories about her precocious son, Alex.

"One day when Alex was about 3 or 4, he was riding next to his dad in the car. They were both silent, presumably listening to the radio, when, out of the blue, Alex says: 'Dad, how *does* that cow get over the moon?'

"Just goes to show that children ponder the complexities of life we adults take for granted."

Chris of West St. Paul: "About a month ago, two longtime friends and I were meeting for dinner in Eden Prairie, and one of them, Joanne of Le Sueur, related this conversation that she and her little 4-year-old son, Mark, had:

"He had said: 'Cow pies are really cows' poop—right?'

"And she had answered him: 'That's right, honey.'

"And he had responded: 'Well, what I want to know is: Who *eats* them?'"

Becky of Cottage Grove: "A few years back, my son and I were driving out to Afton, to an apple orchard, and we saw two cows doing it on a farm.

"And he said: 'Look, Mom! They're playin' leapfrog!'"

Maggie of St. Paul: "My family runs a beef operation in Iowa, and I was walking with my nephew, who was about 7, through the cattle yards. I could see he was really staring, taking it all in.

"There were two steers mounting each other *[Bulletin Board reports: Yes, they do]*, and I knew he was gonna ask me about it, and I was gonna have to explain sexuality—and not only sexuality, but castration, homosexuality . . . I really didn't think I was up for it.

[Bulletin Board notes: Imagine how the steers feel.]

"So he's staring, taking it in, and finally he turns to me and says: 'Look, Margaret! The steers are poppin' wheelies!'"

Barb of St. Paul: "My son Timmy was just 11 when he died in 1982. Even though I still miss him a lot, he left us a lot of happy— and pretty often, pretty funny—memories.

"One of my favorites started with a trip he made to a farm when he was only 5 or 6 years old, with a group from school. They learned all about how goats give milk, and that cheese can be made from that milk—which led us to a discussion of a lot of other animals that give milk, including people, which then led us to a discussion of where babies come from. I gave him a simple, truthful answer to the question of where babies come from, and he seemed satisfied and walked away.

"A couple weeks later, he came to me and asked me: 'Where do babies come from?'

"I said: 'Well, don't you remember? We talked about that the day you went to the farm.'

"He looked me square in the eye, planted both hands on his hips and said: 'Well, you don't think I believe *that*, do you?'"

New Mom of St. Paul: "I have a 4½-year-old son and a new, 8-week-old baby. One day, driving in the car, my son asked me: 'Mom, how'd the baby get in your tummy?'

"I very gingerly started to explain that Papa put a seed there, and it got with Mom's egg, and it grew, and the baby came out. And I was waiting for some other question, like how the seed got there, but my 4-year-old just looked at me and went: 'Naaaaaah!'

"He didn't believe it for a minute."

Karen S. of South St. Paul: "When my oldest daughter, Lisa, was about 8 or 9 years old, she came home from the neighbors' house—she had friends next-door who were older girls, 10 and 12—and she seemed quite agitated.

"She said: 'Mom, where do babies come from?'

"I was kind of taken aback, but I said: 'Lisa, well, you know I told you where babies come from.'

"And she said: 'No, I mean: Where do they really *come* from?'

"And I said: 'Well, you really seem upset, honey. What's the problem?'

"And she said: 'Cindy and Vicki told me something so *ishy*, and Mom, I told them: "My dad might do something like that, but I know my mother *never* would."'"

K.M. of Stillwater: "This past Christmas, our 7-year-old daughter was the Virgin Mary in the Sunday-school Christmas play. One of her lines read: 'How can this be, seeing that I know not a man?' We explained to her that the word 'virgin' and also that line she had to say both meant that Mary had never had sex, so that she could not be pregnant—and it was a miracle that God caused so that Jesus could be born.

"She seemed to understand this explanation and was a wonderful Mary in the play.

"About a month later, while we were brushing our teeth, she turned to me with a knowing look and said: 'Mom, you and Dad have had sex ... twice.'

"I didn't have the heart to say a thing."

Carol of Winona: "I'm a single parent, and my daughter is 8. She desperately wants a baby brother or sister. She went into the kitchen last week and made, as an experiment, some 'pregnancy juice' for me—which consisted of water, food coloring, cookie sprinkles and mashed banana. She brought it to me about an hour later and asked me to drink it—and explained to me that now I could get pregnant without needing a man.

"After I refused to drink it, she said: 'But Mommy, how will I know if it works?'"

BULLETIN BOARD NOTES: A scientist is born.

Leticia of St. Paul: "I have a cousin Anthony, who's 7 years old, and he asked my friend Monica, who's pregnant: 'How do you get pregnant?'

"Monica says: 'Go ask your mom.'

"He says: 'No, Monica, really! How do you get pregnant?'

"She says: 'No, really, Anthony, go ask your mom.'

"So he came up to me and asked me: 'How do you get pregnant?'

"I said: 'Well, you have to kiss for a very long time.'

"He said: 'No. Don't lie to me. I know how you get pregnant.'

"And I asked him: 'How?'

"He said: 'You have to kiss twice a day.'

"And I said: 'Oh, really?'

"He said: 'Yeah.'

"And I said: 'Where did you hear this from?'

"He said: 'Hey. I *do* watch "Oprah." ' "

Gen of St. Paul: "This isn't quite a cute kid story—'cause this kid is 16. He's having difficulty in Biology, so I thought I'd take a look and maybe talk about the material in the genetics chapter.

"So when I see him, I says: 'Who is this guy Mendel?'

"And he looks at me and says: 'Why? Did he call?'

"I see we have a long way to go in Biology."

Ellie of Cottage Grove: "I had to call in a cute kid story just to annoy the people that hate 'em.

"Yesterday, we were listening to Radio AAHS, and there was a song on there called 'We Don't Play With Bruno 'Cause Bruno Is a Dweeb.' I was listening to this with my 5-year-old son—and before people call in and ask how I could let my child listen to this, it really is a nice song; they find out that Bruno's a nice kid at the end, and they play with him anyway—and anyway, after the song was over, my son said: 'Mom, what does that mean?'

"I tried to explain: A dweeb is like a dork, a nerd, someone who's silly.

"And he gave me one of those 5-year-old withering my-mother-is-a-complete-idiot stares, shook his head and said: 'I know *that!* What's a Bruno?' "

JB's Wife: "On Saturday, my 7-year-old son, Ben, had his friend over to spend the afternoon. The two boys were in the living room playing Monopoly, and Garrett wanted to trade some properties with Ben.

"Ben came into the kitchen and asked his older sister, Rachel, what she thought about it. When Rachel told him she didn't think he should make the trade, Ben marched back into the living room and very indignantly told Garrett: 'I'm not stupid, you know!' "

Laurel of White Bear Lake: "This had to be about 20 years ago, when my husband and my daughter were visiting my folks. My daughter Deanna was about 4, and my little sister Georgia was about 5 or 6.

"Georgia had this joke that she'd just heard; it was a really cute knock-knock joke, and it went: 'Knock-knock.' 'Who's there?' 'Old lady.' 'Old lady who?' 'I didn't know you could yodel!'

"Well, Georgia had to tell somebody, and there were these little girls out in the porch, and we grownups were sitting inside and could hear them. Georgia starts out: 'Knock-knock.' And Deanna says: 'Who's there?' And Georgia says: 'Grandma.' And Deanna says: 'Grandma who?' And Georgia says: 'I didn't know you could yodel!'—and they're out there laughing their heads off!

"And, of course, we adults are inside, about dyin' ourselves."

Grandma of Wisconsin: "When my granddaughter started kindergarten, they asked the parents to bring the children in on a Friday for about an hour or so, so they could find their room and meet their teacher. Rachel and her mother did this.

"Then, on Monday morning, my daughter went to waken Rachel, and she says: 'C'mon! Get up! We've gotta get going!'

"And sleepy little Rachel says: 'Where are we going?'

"And her mother says: 'School!'

"And Rachel says: 'Again?' "

Fife's Wife of Austin: "My mom is just the neatest person. She used to be a teacher, and part of her will always remain a teacher and a mom for the rest of her life. She is very wrapped up in her children, her grandchildren and, now, her great-grandchildren.

"This fall, her oldest great-grandson entered kindergarten. She kept thinking about him all week and couldn't wait to find out how things went. She was especially concerned about this little guy riding the big school bus all by himself.

"Finally, Sunday arrived, and when she saw him after church, she bent over and asked, 'Well, Timothy, what was the bus ride like?' A man of few words, he looked up at her with big eyes and said: 'Wild!'

" 'And how was your first week of school?' she continued.

" 'Well,' he said with a hint of disgust in his voice, 'I've been going for a long time already, and I haven't even learned to read yet.' "

Marilyn of St. Paul: "About 18 years ago, when our daughter and I went to her one-on-one kindergarten orientation at Parkway School, her teacher was telling us all about how her half-day would be spent and discussing curriculum with me.

"The kindergarten room had its own little lavatory, and near the end of the interview, the teacher, trying to familiarize our daughter with the new facilities, said to Jennifer: 'Jennifer, can you show your mommy how you flush the toilet and wash your hands?'

"To which my daughter politely but tentatively responded: 'But . . . my mommy already knows how to do that.' "

Michele of St. Paul, whose son is in first grade: "He was really eager to boast to me of his new accomplishment: knowing the *whole* Pledge of Allegiance.

"He said it: 'I pledge allegiance to the flag of the United States of America, and to the republic for which it stands—one nation, under God, indivisible, with liberty and justice for all. You may sit down.'

"I thought they'd probably added a few words since I was in school."

Beth of White Bear Lake: "We were sitting at dinner the other night, and the kids were talking about their day at school.

"Rachel, who's 5, was talking about her day at kindergarten. She was telling me: 'Mom, we learned a really important game today!'

"I said: 'Oh, you did?'

"And she said: 'Yes. It has two really, really important rules.'

"I said: 'Oh, really? Well, what are they?'

"She said: 'The first rule is: Always pay attention.'

" 'That's a really good rule,' I said. 'What's the second one?'

"She said: 'Ummmm . . . I forget.' "

Manly Man of Eagan: "I wanted to pass along a story I heard at church recently from a kindergarten-teacher friend of mine. She was telling her new students the rules of the classroom. When she got to the instructions about how to take care of their bodily needs, she told them that if they needed to go to the bathroom, they should just raise their hand with two fingers showing.

"Immediately, one of the new students raised his hand, so she called on him to see if he had a question. He said: 'Miss Davies, I just don't understand how that's gonna help.'"

Don of South St. Paul: "The other night, our first-grader and second-grader were at the table practicing their spelling words.

"It was the second-grader's turn to ask the first-grader to spell a word. The word was 'WHEN.' She asked him to spell the word, but there was silence.

"He then quickly got up from his chair and headed out of the room. She asked where he was going, and he replied: 'I need to poop!'

"She said: 'WHEN.'

"On the dead run, he said: *'Right now!'*"

Kathy of Blaine: "We just returned from a trip north. We were at a cabin for a week, and my daughter one day nicely asked for a glass of milk from her dad.

"Her dad got her a glass, put it in front of her and started to pour—and looked at her and said: 'OK, say when.'

"She looked at him out of the corner of her eye and said: 'Today!'

"She's 5. I got the biggest kick out of that."

Laurie of St. Paul: "I do child care at a shelter, and last night all eight of the kids were in the kitchen getting a drink.

"One of the 4-year-old girls accidentally bumped into another kid and made him spill water all over the floor.

"I looked at her and asked: 'What do you say?'

"She thought for a second and then said: 'Oops?'"

Debbie of Inver Grove Heights: "Back when my son was 4 years old, he had to go to the doctor for his first physical. The lab technician gave him a little cup and said: 'Now, Eric, you have to go and go potty in this.'

"Eric was in the bathroom for a while, and then he came out and said: 'Mom, I can't go potty in that.'

"I went into the bathroom to find out what the problem was. There he had that little cup sitting on the floor—and he was trying to go potty in it. And if that doesn't beat all, I don't know what does."

BULLETIN BOARD NOTES: Curiosity got the best of us—our journalistic instinct kicked in, unaccountably—so we called to verify that we were getting the proper (so to speak) picture here.

When Debbie and the lab technician said "go potty," they did, in fact, mean "urinate"—just in case you, too, wondered.

We were thinking: If she'd meant not "urinate" but the alternative, that would beat all.

Speak plainly to your children, people.

Terry of St. Paul: "I took my son to the doctor, and my 7-year-old daughter tagged along.

"My son had to go to the lab to have some tests done, and he asked me what they would be doing. I said: 'Well, you might have to pee in a cup, and they may do a finger stick.'

"When we sat down in the waiting room, my daughter looked at me and sort of sighed and dropped her shoulders and said: 'I'm *so* hungry. Can I have a finger stick, too?'"

John Jansen of Minneapolis: "My 2-year-old daughter and 6-year-old son went to the doctor for the 6-year-old's checkup.

"The doctor put a stethoscope on his chest, and my 2-year-old said: 'My turn! My turn!'

"The doctor hit his knee; the 2-year-old said: 'My turn! My turn!'

"The doctor poked his finger to get some blood; the 2-year-old said: 'Not *my* turn, Mommy.'"

Mama of Lakeland: "My 6-year-old daughter's teacher sent a note home with her yesterday, and I read it out loud to her.

"Karen beamed at the comments about how she was adjusting well to first grade, making friends. But then a suggestion that she needs to work on using a softer indoor voice made Karen yell, in her best Marjorie Main/Ma Kettle voice: 'I AM WORKING ON IT!'"

E-I-E-I-O of St. Paul: "My 10-year-old came home yesterday and said that their teacher had them write out New Year's resolutions. She described what her sheet looks like: all of the colors and designs she put on it, and everything.

"I said: 'Well, that's great—but what's your New Year's resolution?'

"She said: 'I said that I'm gonna spend more time with my little sister.'

"And I said: 'Well, that's wonderful! That's really neat, and I bet your little sister's gonna like that.'

"And my 10-year-old put her hands on her hips and mustered all of her sisterly love and said: 'She . . . *better.*'"

Louise of East Bethel: "When my daughter, Laura, who's now 8, was about 5, she was saying her prayers at night—and her brother had made up a little blurb at the end of his prayers, where he would say: 'Now I lay me down to sleep, I pray the Lord my soul to keep. Angels guide me through the night and wake me in the morning light'—and then he'd say: 'Take back all my sins and lies. I'll try not to lie again.'

"Laura decided she was going to copy this, but she thought she should add something different. She said: 'Take back all my sins and lies. I might lie again.'

"I looked at her real strange, and I said: 'Well, what do you mean by that?'

"And she said: 'Well, you never know, Mom.'"

M.J. of Maplewood: "Last year for Mother's Day, my grandson gave his mother a card with a list of promises to be done once, upon request—such as 'Cleaning my room without complaining' or 'Carry out the garbage immediately when asked.'

"One promise was: 'I will not fight with my brother for one day.' In parenthesis, he added: 'Unless provoked.'"

Kate C. of Maplewood: "Katie, my 7-year-old, came running down to me, very upset. She told me that my 3-year-old, Casey, had just got done calling her a jerk.

"Casey came running in behind her to innocently explain: 'Not a bad jerk, Katie. A good jerk!'"

The College Girl's Mom of White Bear Lake: "It's my daughter's first year away at school, and remembering all of the cute things she's said and done helps me miss her a little less.

"About five years ago, we were all sitting around the dinner table when my daughter, who was reacting to a comment my son had just made, said: 'Well, I'll bet you're the biggest geek in the class.'

"To which my son replied: 'I am *not* the biggest geek in the class. I'm the second-biggest geek in the class!'"

BULLETIN BOARD REPLIES: Perhaps we're unclear on the concept here, but that's a cute thing your son said, not your daughter.

Oh, well. Perhaps she meant it in a cute way.

Dave of Andover: "Last night, our three sons were doing the dishes, and they started bickering and name-calling—as usual. Their mother told them to knock it off—and if they couldn't say something positive, she didn't want to hear anything at all.

"A few seconds later, you could hear our 10-year-old say: 'Well, I'm positive you're ugly'—which cracked 'em all up and broke the tension.

"They all lived happily ever after—or for at least two, three minutes."

Tom of St. Paul: "When I was almost 10, we were remodeling our house—so we were forced for a time to do our dishes in our small bathroom sink.

"My parents went out one evening and asked me to do the dishes. I said: 'But where will I rinse them?' And my mom said: 'You're smart. You'll figure it out.'

"Sure enough, I did. My parents returned home to find me washing the dishes in the sink and rinsing them in the toilet.

"All I can say is: I'm glad they caught me."

Neb of Eagan: "My wife was feeding our two little kids—my 2½-year-old daughter and my 8-month-old son. Kids that age are pretty messy—especially my son; he had food all over his face and his hair and all over the high chair.

"My wife was cleaning him up, and she said: 'Boy, you're messy, Nathan. Looks like I'm gonna have to pop you in the tub.'

"So my wife took my son back to the bedroom and undressed him and brought him into the bathroom—and there was my daughter, sittin' in the tub, with her clothes on.

"She said to my wife: 'I want pop in the tub, too.'"

Robyn's Mom of St. Paul: "Robyn recently turned 6, and she's quite proud of how grown-up she's getting to be. The other day, she was drinking some grape pop, and after making a rather unladylike noise, she said, quite delightedly: 'Mom! I had a purple burp!'

"Things have been a little rocky for me lately, and I just thank God for giving me a little girl who makes me laugh and brings sunshine into my life."

Anita of Stillwater: "I was in the bathroom, and I saw a watermelon seed on the floor—so I picked it up and dropped it in the toilet, while I was still sitting there.

"And being the mother of a 4½-year-old, I'm never alone to do these things—and when I got up, my son, Sean, said: 'Wow! There's a little-bitty poop in the toilet!'

"I said: 'No, that's not a poop; it's a watermelon seed. I picked it up off the floor.'

"And he just gave me this horrified look, and he kept staring at me, and finally he said: 'Why did you *eat* it?'"

Bridget of Mahtomedi: "I was at a fast-food restaurant today with my 4-year-old, and I bumped into an acquaintance I hadn't seen in a couple years. She was pregnant, and I said: 'Oh, you're having another baby!'

"She says: 'Yes, I ate a watermelon seed.'

"My 4-year-old perks up right away and says: 'A *white* seed or a *black* seed?'"

Gramma Barb of St. Paul: "When my son Dave was 4 years old, I told him that my friend Louise was going to have a brand-new baby. After a thoughtful moment, he said: 'What's she gonna do with the old one?'"

Rebecca of Roseville—three months pregnant, but not yet showing: "Last night, my husband and I were having dinner with some friends of ours. Our friends' 7-year-old son was looking at me, and all of a sudden he said: 'Mommy, where's Rebecca's baby?'

"And she said: 'Remember? I told you her baby's in her tummy.'

"And then he said: 'Well, where's the big bump that the baby goes in?'"

Julie of St. Paul: "My son was about 5. My daughter is older than him, and her and I were talking about a vacation we had been on; I had been pregnant with him at the time. And he had to pipe up, as always, and say: 'I remember that! I remember that!'

"So I took some time out to explain: 'No, you couldn't remember. You were in my stomach. I was pregnant with you then. You weren't born yet.'

"And he said: 'Yes, I remember. I was peekin' out the hole!'"

Franci of Woodbury: "Several years ago, my husband, our 3-year-old daughter, Traci, and I went to Disney World. At that time, I was pregnant with our daughter Toni.

"One evening, while entertaining guests, we started visiting about the wonderful time we had at Disney World. Traci, now 8, very enthusiastically said that her favorite part of Disney World was when she got to talk to Mickey Mouse.

"Caught up in the excitement, Toni—now 5—shouted out that her favorite part was Pirates of the Caribbean (which was not yet built at the time we were there). Traci looked at her with the disgust only an older sister can give and said: 'You weren't even born then. Mom was still pregnant with you.'

"Toni piped up and said: 'I knewed that, but I was looking through her belly button.'"

Shorty of Lake Elmo: "Tonight for supper, we were having tacos, and I mentioned that it was one of my favorite foods. My son Tyler, who's 4½ years old, said that was one of his favorite foods, too.

"I said: 'Well, I ate a lot of tacos when I was pregnant with you.'

"He says: 'What does that mean?'

"And I said: 'Well, when you were in my tummy—that means I was pregnant with you.'

"And he said: 'Oh, yeah! I remember the tacos dropping on my head!'"

A.L. of parts hereabouts: "A girl I work with is six months pregnant. Her little boy is 4 years old, and she was saying how the baby's going to start kicking, but he hasn't started kicking yet.

"She was getting dressed, just sitting there, and she hadn't put her shirt on yet, and he came up to her and put his stomach against her stomach and said: 'Now the baby can kick me, too.' Cute."

Anonymous man: "My wife is into her fourth month of pregnancy. Our 5-year-old daughter decided to play doctor and put her toy stethoscope in her ears and listened to her mom's heartbeat.

"She then says: 'I'm going to listen to the baby's heartbeat.' After a minute, she comes back and says: 'Dad, I just heard the baby [expel a posterior breeze].'

"The wife and I are still laughing."

Grandma Up North: "My daughter called me today. She's in Chicago, and she's very pregnant—due any day.

"She was lying on the couch, rubbing her stomach, and her little boy, who is 2, came up and said: 'Mommy, the baby ate your belly button!' "

Molly's Mom: "Molly is getting ready to leave for college. Her dad and I are feeling nostalgic about the funny little girl who used to live with us.

"When Molly was 2 years old, her brother was born. We had given her a few basic facts about the arrival procedure. One day, she was processing some of the information and asked me: 'When the babies sneak out of your fur, are they flat?' "

Molly of St. Paul: "When I was expecting my third baby, last October, my almost-4-year-old daughter was asking me how the baby would get out of my tummy. Well, I explained the whole process to her, and after she'd thought it through, she said, very sincerely: 'Hmmm. Sounds like a tight squeeze.' "

Jackie of Oakdale: "I'm pregnant with my second child, and the baby's really movin' around a lot now. So I lifted my shirt to show my 3-year-old daughter, Lauren, the movement and pointed to where you could see it.

"She said: 'No, Mommy. That's not where he is'—and pointed to my belly button and said: 'He's in the hole!'

"Kinda makes you wonder where, exactly, she thinks he's gonna emerge from."

BULLETIN BOARD REPLIES: Anyone who didn't know better would find the little girl's theory every bit as plausible as the truth.

We've seen it, for heaven's sake—and we still don't believe it!

The Reading Doc of Rochester: "Years ago, when our No. 4 child (The Incredible Twerp) was just an infant, my wife (Rosie the Riveter) had a neighbor over for coffee.

"It was time to nurse the Twerp, and Rosie proceeded to do just that, with the usual discreet covering of baby.

"Apparently the little crib blanket she was using as a 'cover' was not covering as well as she thought. The neighbor's 5-year-old, who had been playing in the other room, happened to come into the kitchen, stared at Rosie and Twerp, started to return to the other room, then stopped and said: 'Hey, lady! Do you know that kid's chewin' on your thing?'"

Linda of Cottage Grove: "I'm baby-sitting my 3-year-old, and I have a new baby in the house. His name is Aaron.

"I was nursing Aaron one day, and Ian looked at me and said: 'Aunt Linda, is Aaron eating your shirt?' So cute."

Linda of Eagan: "Many years ago, in a more modest—not to say more uptight—time, my mother was breastfeeding me. Behind closed doors, of course.

"My twin 7-year-old brothers burst in and wanted to know what she was doing. She managed to blurt out something about: 'Well, you know how cows give milk. Well, mommies do, too.'

"And after a moment of stunned silence, my brother John said: 'You mean you've been eatin' *grass?*'"

Young Little Six of St. Paul: "When my mom and dad brought my little sister home from the hospital, my then-4-year-old brother was asked to get the scissors to cut off the hospital band.

"All of the sudden, we heard my brother say to my father: 'Hey, Dad! Mom needs the scissors so she can cut off the baby's price tag.'"

Grandma of St. Paul: "My granddaughter and I were looking at her pictures—and 'Oh, here's Mama when you were still in her tummy' and 'Oh, here's another picture of Mama when you were still in her tummy.'

"The next pictures were of a brand-new baby, and she said: 'Oh, here I am! Mama finally let me get out!'"

Lori of Lino Lakes: "Last night, my 4-year-old son, Zakk, and I spent the evening watching home movies.

"We were watching the movie of the day he was born, and it begins with him being weighed and measured in the hospital. Zakk goes: 'Why is there that black stuff on the bottom of my feet?' I told him it was the ink they used to take his footprints.

"Later on in the movie, Daddy's changing Zakk's first dirty diaper, and Zakk goes: 'Why is my butt so black?' I told him he was having a diaper changed—to which he replied: 'Oh! I thought maybe they needed a buttprint, too.'"

Iced Tea Judy of Eagan: "I have a 2-year-old, and we're working on toilet-training right now.

"I asked her: 'Honey, do you *like* wearing diapers?'

"And she said: 'Yes.'

"And I said: 'Aw, but *babies* wear diapers. What do big girls wear?'

"And she said: 'Big diapers.'"

Beth of parts undisclosed: "I'm calling to tell about something that happened up in Ely.

"My grandson Charlie and I were walking early in the morning, around town, and there were several huge, tall pine trees that were felled. They had been cut down for some reason.

"I said: 'Charlie, I wonder why those big pine trees are all down.'

"And he said: 'Maybe somebody's using too much toilet paper.'"

P.P.R. of Owatonna: 'My 2-year-old daughter is currently working on potty training. It takes a while. She'll do a little job, and then she wants to get up and inspect—see how things are going. It's 'Daddy, I made a pooper,' 'Daddy, I did this,' 'Daddy, I did that.'

"Well, we're waitin', and it's gettin' to be kind of a long job here. She's playin' with her little sticker book at the same time. Well, I've got one on my finger—a little sticker—and as she gets up to check, I toss it into her little potty chair.

"And she's so proud: 'Daddy! Look! Daddy, I made a sticker!'"

Scott of Hudson, Wis.: "I was walking home from school one day when my 4-year-old neighbor walked up to me. He was just so happy to see me. I then noticed the big, round sticker he was wearing on his shirt. It said: 'I just got my library card!'

"I read the whole sticker out loud. Exact words.
"Then he said: 'Me, too!' "

John of St. Paul: "So I'm driving along in my car today with my 4-year-old son, and a song comes on the radio. My son is really into music, for some reason, and he says to me: 'Dad, who's singin' this song?'
"I said: 'U2.'
"He goes: 'I'm not singin' this song!' "

Betty of St. Paul: "I was taking my son to the store, and he found a paper by the steps. He put it under his arm and said: 'I the mailman.'
"I wanted to correct him, and I said: 'No, I'm the mailman.'
"And he indignantly said to me: 'No, you not!' he said. 'I the mailman!' "

The Cheese Lady of the East Side: "I was driving home the other day with my 2½-year-old son, and out of nowhere, he says: 'Mom, Grandma doesn't know my name. She thinks I'm a pie.'
"I said: 'A pie? What do you mean?'
"He said: 'Well, she calls me Honey Pie—but I'm *not* a pie. I'm a little boy.' "

Maggie of North St. Paul: "A few months ago, when my 3-year-old grandson was leaving after a visit, I said: 'See you later, alligator.'
"And he said: 'No. No, Grandma. I'm *Matthew.*' "

Pat Pearson of White Bear: "Andrew, our 3½-year-old, was just developing a cold and was having a conversation with his Opa (grandpa).
"Opa said: 'Boy, Andrew, you're a little hoarse today.'
"Andrew laughed, looked up at Opa and said: 'I'm not a horse. I'm a little kid.' "

Kim of White Bear Lake: "When my nephew was about 4 years old, he was over at my parents' house playing around like a little detective, wearing one of those little plastic sheriff's badges. I was there waiting for a friend to show up. When my friend did show up, I wasn't quite ready, so my friend was forced to stand around and wait for me.

"When my friend saw my nephew's little plastic badge, he asked him: 'Oh my, are you a sheriff?'

"My little nephew looked at my friend as if he were stupid and said: 'No, I'm just a little kid!'"

Catherine of Tarragon: "A while back, my husband and I went to visit our grandsons. In response to our knock, Brian, who was then 6 years old, came to the door wearing a black-and-yellow Batman sweatshirt.

"Grandpa said to him: 'Hi there, Brian. Are you Batman today?'

"Brian replied: 'No, Grandpa. I am a *good* man.'

"And he looked so *sad*."

Scott's Happy Wife of St. Paul: "The 4-year-old I take care of told me his underwear were a little wet today. In the bathroom, I said: 'It looks more than a little wet. You're . . . pretty wet.'

"He said: 'No! I'm *handsome* wet.'"

Wheezer's Ma of Little Canada: "My 2-year-old and I play a little game where I'll say 'Your jacket,' 'Your shoes,' or whatever, and he responds with 'My jacket,' 'My shoes,' etc.

"This morning, I saw him reach up to the refrigerator and pull down a lovely Hallmark given to me by a dear friend named Yoshimi. As he tackled it to the ground, I very gingerly pulled it from his hot little hands and said: 'No, no. You'll ruin our nice card from Yoshimi.'

"His response: '*My* shimi.'"

Dave Unmacht of Prior Lake: "I have a 3-year-old daughter who is beginning to watch the Disney classics. She's watched *The Great Mouse Detective, Dumbo, Beauty and the Beast, Pinocchio*—those sorts of things—on the VCR.

"*Dumbo* was the one we most recently found for her. Tuesday night she watched it—and wanted to watch it again. The Twins were playing Toronto, and I didn't want to watch *Dumbo* again.

"She came over and sat on my lap and told me she 'lubs' me—and gave me that innocent look and said: 'Oh, let's watch it, Daddy.'

"I looked at her and said: 'No, Daddy doesn't want to watch it.'

"And she said: 'Pretend it's a ballgame, Daddy'—and she gave me that look.

"Sure enough, we watched *Dumbo*—again. And we missed the ballgame for that night."

BULLETIN BOARD NOTES: It was a great game to miss. But then again, how could a Twins game—or pretty much any ballgame, really—hope to compete with "that look" from a 3-year-old girl?

Rich of Arden Hills: "My wife was recently gone on a business trip, so it became my job to put my 6½-year-old daughter to bed.

"After I had put her to bed, she called me into the bedroom and said: 'You know, when I'm not tired, usually Mom sings me a lullaby. But,' she said, 'you're a guy! So why don't you just sing 'Take Me Out to the Ballgame.'"

Midlife Mom of New Richmond, Wis.: "My 7-year-old was sitting on the back steps with his ball and glove, waiting for his dad to finish mowing the lawn. I felt sorry for the little guy, so I got my mitt and asked him if he wanted to play with me.

"He looked at me for a long while and then asked: 'Have you improved any since the last time we played?'

"The best thing is: He let me play with him, anyway."

Lance of Minnetonka: "I took my child, Wes, to his first Twins game, and through the luck of connections, we got tickets in the very front row. While we were there, the guy sitting next to us, who's had season tickets since 1965, called out to one of the White Sox players to throw us a ball because it was my son's first game—a little 4-year-old.

"Ozzie Guillen of the White Sox threw a ball. Surprised me; knocked my popcorn all over the place; I dropped the ball back on the field. He threw it up again. I caught it, handed it to my son. And while I was picking up my popcorn, my son, being the good boy he is, threw the ball back on the field.

"There was no one left on the field, and it rolled all the way to the first-base line.

"So we never got the ball."

Amy of Stillwater: "While playing catch with my 3-year-old niece, Annalise, I noticed she was making great efforts and catching the ball successfully. I complimented her and asked: 'How did you learn to catch so well?'

" 'My grandma,' she says.

" 'Which one,' I ask. (She has two great-grandmas, Bev and Kay.) And she proceeds to tell me, while holding up her two fingers: 'I have two grandmas.' Of course, I know this, but she continues to count out her grandmas, one on each finger: 'One grandma, two grandmas.'

"So I ask: 'Which one showed you how to catch?'

" 'This one!' she exclaims, pointing to her second finger."

Pat of St. Paul: "I've got 2½-year-old twin daughters. We're try-ing to teach them a little rudimentary arithmetic.

"My daughter, Laura, was standing there, and my wife held up five fingers and said: 'How many fingers is this?'

"She said: 'Five.'

"So my wife held up both hands and said: 'How many fingers is this?'

"And Laura looked at the other hand and said: 'Five.'

"And my wife said: 'No, Laura. When I've got this hand up and this hand up, how many fingers is that?'

"And without missing a beat, Laura said: 'A lot.' "

Grandpa Bob of the East Side: "Annie, who is a day-care per-son, took our two sons over to a park in White Bear Lake to swing. While pushing Andy, who's 5½, and Matt, who's 3½, she observed a grandpa pushing his grandson on a swing next to them. He was counting each push: 'One, two, three, four, five and . . . shoo!'—which was an accelerated shove.

"After a number of these repetitions, Matt got off his swing and went over to the grandpa and pulled on his shirt and said: 'Man? Man? Six comes after five, not shoo!' "

I Can Count of Woodbury: "When I was young, my mom for some reason got mad at me, so she said: 'You can go sit in the cor-ner. I'll give you three seconds to explain what you were doing.' And then she counted to three: 'One, two, three'—and I was real young, and I started counting: 'Four, five, six' all the way up to 10, and she was so proud of me that she forgot the punishment."

Cindy of South St. Paul: "The other day, I made a meal that my two older children didn't like, and they told me about it. But my youngest daughter, who's 5, said that, well, she liked it.

"My oldest son said: 'Well, you don't count.'

"And she proceeded to say: 'Yes, I do! One, two, three, four, five.'"

Frank of Merriam Park: "My wife and I were out the other day to Kohl's department store in Roseville, and there were three cute little-girl mannequins, all dressed up pretty.

"I called over to my wife: 'Hey, honey, look at these! Aren't they cute?' And just at that time, there was a little girl about the same size standing beside them. She looked at me, and I said: 'You, too.'

"She looked back at me and said: 'No. I 3!'"

Keri Olson: "On the Thursday before my wedding, I went to Target with my sister Lori and her two kids, Brandon (4½) and Justin (3½), to get some last-minute things for the wedding and honeymoon.

"Lori had Brandon in her cart; they went one way. I had Justin in my cart, and we went the other way.

"We were looking at the aerobics wear, which is near the panty-hose section. I was trying to decide between two pair of aerobics shorts, when all of a sudden I hear Justin yell: 'Auntie Keri, look! There are people stuck in that wall over there!'

"He was looking at those models of legs they have on the walls to show the different shades of pantyhose."

Jessica of Litchfield: "I baby-sit for this really nice family, and last night I went there for supper.

"They were telling me that Dr. W. and Grant—he's 14—went hunting and found this deer skull. So they took it home, and now it's in their front lawn.

"And Michelle, who's 3, asked their mom: 'Mom, what *is* that?'

"Mrs. W. goes: 'That's a deer.'

"'Is it dead?'

" 'Yes, it's dead.'

" 'Well, is he in heaven?'

" 'Yeah, the deer's probably in heaven.'

" 'Well, is it walking around?'

" 'Yeah, probably.'

" 'Well, don't you think he *needs* that?' "

Lisa of Apple Valley: "Several years ago, my husband was in chiropractic college, and I was teaching elementary music and private piano lessons in the evenings to make ends meet.

"We lived in a small apartment; our piano was next to my husband's desk—which held his books and notes—as well as a life-size plastic spine, suspended from a metal stand.

"During one lesson, a 7-year-old student was visibly distracted by the spine. When she stopped playing to ask 'What is that?,' I told her: 'Oh, it's just my husband's.'

"Well, she looked back at her music—and then asked: 'Did it hurt him when they took it out?' "

Donelle of Roseville: "Several years ago, I had a complete hysterectomy. I had endometriosis. I was relating the story to a friend on the telephone, and I said: 'The doctors took everything—the appendix, the ovaries, everything.'

"When I got off the phone, my little boy says: 'Mama, did they leave your heart?' "

D.B. of St. Paul: "My little grandson recently moved away, to Grand Rapids. He came back to visit about a month after he left, and I said to him: 'Jeremy, Grandma's heart ached for you when you were gone. Did your heart ache for Grandma?'

"He looked at me and said: 'No, Grandma—but my leg hurt.' "

Alan of Rochester: "My wife was explaining to my 6-year-old daughter, Jessica, how the family was related. To see if she had grasped the concept, my wife asked: 'When you have a baby, what will I be?'

"Jessica replied: 'Grandma.'

" 'And what will Daddy be?'

"Jessica replied: 'Grandpa.'

"'And how about your sister? What will she be to the baby?'

"To that, Jessica replied, with a big smile on her face: 'Baby-sitter!'"

BULLETIN BOARD OBSERVES: She's grasped the concept perfectly!

Becca of Frogtown: "I was baby-sitting for three sisters the other night, and when the parents came home, the youngest daughter, Abby—she's 4—went running to the door, yelling: 'Mommy! The girl's still here! She stayed and played with us all night!'"

Mom of Little Canada: "My 70-year-old mother does day care for my 3-year-old son, Adam.

"During the day, my mother must have been working on him to use good manners—because later in the evening, when I was washing dishes, Adam entered the kitchen and announced that he'd tooted. Then he continued to tell me: 'Excuse me. That's good manners.'

"He briefly left the room, only to return minutes later to explain that he'd just had a little air, and that was all—but continued to say: 'But Mom, sometimes Grandma has *lots* of air.'

"I looked at him, and we both burst out laughing.

"I want to say: Thanks, Mom. You're doing a wonderful job."

Granny Kay of St. Paul: "My 3-year-old grandson, Christopher, was sitting on the couch just now, and he [expelled a posterior breeze].

"He said: 'Uh-oh, I [expelled a posterior breeze].'

"And I said: 'What do you say?'

"And he said: 'Pig.'

"And I said: 'That's not what you say, Christopher.'

"And he said: 'Uh-huh. That's what my mom says to my dad every time *he* [expels a posterior breeze].'"

Red of Hastings: "Years ago, I had a friend who, every time he [expelled a posterior breeze], would say: 'Oops, stepped on a frog.'

"One day, I was up visiting, and his 4-year-old son and I were out walking in the woods, and he looked at me and said: 'You know, every time Pop steps on a frog, he [expels a posterior breeze].'"

Chris of St. Paul: "While shopping with my 3-year-old son at Kmart last Saturday, he proceeded to pass gas in the automotive aisle. It was particularly smelly flatulence.

"Two people who were standing nearby needed some things from the shelf where we were standing, so they had to walk into the midst of our [posterior breeze]. I didn't want them to think that I had done it, so I said to my son: 'Michael, now see what happened? You [expelled a posterior breeze] in public, and now these people have to smell it.'

"We went about 10 feet down and stood out of the way; we were waiting for my husband. As we're standing there, these same two people come walking toward us, again!

"My 3-year-old son looked up at the guy and said: 'Hey, mister! Did you have to smell it? Did you smell my [posterior breeze]?'

"He was very proud of himself."

Big Bill of Inver Grove Heights: "My brother was out shopping with his 2-year-old daughter at a local department store—and realized he hadn't seen her for a minute or two. Started to look around—and saw a pile of clothes on the floor. Looked up a hallway just in time to see his very nude daughter run into an open elevator and disappear.

"I think he aged a year as he waited for that elevator to return—which it did, with a rather concerned customer holding the hand of his nude daughter.

"Jessica, I might add, is now 15 years old, blonde and beautiful, and prefers to shop with her clothes on."

J.W. of Roseville: "When my daughter was about 3 years old, she was in the store with me, and the clerk asked her what her name was. My daughter put her arm around me and said: 'My name is Elise, and this is my friend Mommy.'"

Leo Anderson of Eau Claire, Wis., about a visit to the toy department with his young grandson Daniel of Cedar Rapids, Iowa: "We're walking toward the checkout counter, and I hear him muttering. I look around. No one is near.

" 'Daniel, who are you talking to?'

" 'I'm talking to myself.'

" 'Why are you talking to yourself?'
" 'I just want to know what I'm thinking.' "

Maya of Spring Valley, Wis.: "The other day, I was driving my sister to school, and we saw a man with his car broken down by the side of the road. By the time we got turned around and came back to where he was, he was gone.

"My sister said: 'Well, that's OK. Maybe he'll be there tomorrow.' "

Chuck of Minneapolis: "About kids' misperceptions of things: Our now 5-year-old was talking to her mom a couple years ago, when Desert Storm was going on, and her mom was saying that she was gonna take her to Target to do some shopping. And Carrie said that she didn't think they could go to Target, because she'd heard on the radio that all the Targets had been bombed."

Stacy of Forest Lake: "Recently, I was taking my son down to Target in Shoreview. We were driving on 35W, and he was asking me questions about why the people behind us were going where they were going, who they were going to see.

"I told him I didn't know, because we didn't know them, and he said: 'Well, Mommy, if we don't know them, why are they following us?' "

Mary of Newport: "My brother and my mom were goin' down the road in the family's brown pickup truck, and my brother waved to another brown pickup truck going by.

"My mom says: 'Who are you waving to?'
"And my brother says: 'Oh! I thought it was us.' "

Anonymous man: "About two years ago, when my grandson was about 9 or 10, he and I were going fishing, and we were driving up the highway toward Sandstone—and in the process, discussing fishing. And he very seriously says: 'My dad's gonna buy a boat.' And I thought: Now, that's unusual—since I know his father.

"I said: 'Oh, he is? What makes you think that your dad's gonna buy a boat?'
"He says: 'Well, he *told* me the very last thing he was gonna buy is a boat.' "

M.J. of the East Side: "I was going to take my family to the Minnesota Zoo. So I was discussing this with my mate, and I was telling him that there was also a Native American exhibit at the zoo.

"I went into the other room and came back into the living room, and my 6-year-old was very upset. His name is Brandon.

He said: 'Why are we gonna kill birds at the zoo?'

"I said: 'We're not gonna kill birds at the zoo.'

"And he said: 'Yeah, you said we were gonna kill birds at the zoo!'

"And I said: 'Well, OK, I don't think I said that.'

"I was sitting there for a few minutes, and then I started laughing—because I remembered what I had said: 'If we go out there, we can kill two birds with one stone.'"

Laure of the West Side: "My 3-year-old niece, Jennifer, was over the other day. She came out of the playroom holding a musical jack-in-the-box in one arm—and with the other hand, she was trying to push the clown back down into the box and get the lid closed. Well, it wasn't working.

"She looked at me, and she sighed: 'Auntie, could you please help me? I'm havin' a hard time gettin' this weasel back in here.'"

Eve of Buffalo City, Wis.: "I have to tell you about a little 7-year-old who comes to stay with us after school until his mom is done working.

"The first day that he came, it was really blistering hot. We had the air conditioning on, and my husband came in the house—which he usually doesn't do that early in the day. He was sitting on the davenport, so I introduced them. They didn't talk to each other too much.

"The next day, it wasn't so warm, so my husband wasn't in there—and little Joey said: 'Where's that man who was sitting on your davenport yesterday?'"

Soupy of the North End: "Our 5-month-old granddaughter was baptized last Sunday at 9 o'clock Mass.

"Our 2½-year-old granddaughter, Erica, was askin' her mom who was going to be there at church:

"'Grandma?'

" 'Yes.'

" 'Great-grandma?'

" 'Yes.'

" 'Grandpa?'

" 'Yes.'

"Erica thought for a minute and said: 'You mean Grandpa's gonna get off the couch?' "

N of the East Side: "I am a first-grade teacher here in St. Paul.

"Recently, I had a miscarriage. Since my students had been aware of my pregnancy, I needed to explain that the baby had died. After I had read a book that covered explaining miscarriages to children, I set out to do it properly.

"After my explanation, I received the following four questions:

"1. Did you see the baby?

"2. Did it hurt?

"3. Is your baby in heaven?

"4. When is the Christmas party again?"

Young at Heart of Roseville: "I was casting kids in our church for our annual Christmas play, and I was giving out choices, such as Shepherd, Lamb, Villager.

"One 5-year-old boy couldn't decide, so I said: 'Luke, you can be a Villager.'

"He said: 'OK'—and ran over to his parents. Very excited, he said to them: 'Guess *what!* I get to be a mini-van!' "

Sharon's Day Care of Cottage Grove: "Two years ago, I cared for a boy named Roger, who was 4 at the time. Two weeks before Christmas, we were discussing the things we had to do, and I said: 'I need to get a haircut before Christmas.'

"And Roger said: 'I need a bath before Christmas.'

"Then, this year, I made a North Pole for the kids, and I told 'em it's where Santa lives. And Ashley, who is now age 4, says: 'That's where Santa's slaves live, too—right?'

"These kids always give me something to smile about. Merry Christmas."

Kris, Mom of 2 of Stillwater: "Listening to Christmas carols with my son, I asked him how we get a white Christmas.

"Benjamin replied: 'With snow!'

"I then said: 'Great-grandma in Florida doesn't get a white Christmas, because it's green all the time.'

"To which Benjamin exclaimed: 'They have *green snow?*'"

JoAnn of Mahtomedi: "We were singing 'Hark, the Herald Angels Sing,' and after the line 'peace on Earth, and mercy mild,' my little brother Keith, who's 2, says to me: 'You know what? You can *eat* peas.'

"I just thought it was really cute."

JoAnn of Maplewood: "My 3-year-old grandson, Cory, received a new paint set for Christmas. One day, he was telling me all about the pictures he was making, and I said: 'Will you please make Grandma a pretty picture?'

"He said: 'OK.'

"I said: 'Good. I'm going to take it to work and hang it up.'

"After a slight pause, he said: 'Grandma, do you have a *refrigerator* at your work?'"

Elaine of Lakeland: "My mother . . . has told this story so many times: When she was baby-sitting for my kids when they were little, my 3-year-old daughter brought her a Christmas package and was describing it to her: 'It's warm, and it's fuzzy.'

"And the 5-year-old told her: 'You're not supposed to tell.'

"And the 3-year-old answered: 'I didn't say it was a *robe.*'

"That's just my mom's favorite story."

Jeanne of St. Paul: "Another trip down Memory Lane: This happened 37 years ago, when our son Steven was 3 years old.

"We had very little money. My husband was a full-time engineering student at the university; I worked full-time; and my mom took care of Steven, free of charge. We lived in student housing (read: Quonset hut).

"It was Christmastime, and my husband and son went shopping for my gift. When they came home, Steven had to tell me, very proudly, that they'd bought me a secret scarf."

Mother of Many of West St. Paul: "My mom asked the little neighbor boy if he'd been good this year and if Santa was coming. He said Santa *might* come. He'd been pretty good—except for August."

JoAnn of Coon Rapids: "My daughter and son-in-law were doing a practice run-through for the benefit of their 3-year-old son before his first meeting with Santa down at the mall.

"My son-in-law sat on my daughter's lap, and she said: 'Ho-ho-ho! What is your name, little boy?'

"And he answered: 'My name is Ben.'

" 'Ho-ho-ho! And how old are you, Ben?' said Santa.

" 'Well, I'm 41,' said Ben.

" 'Ho-ho-ho!' continued Santa. 'And what would you like for Christmas?'

"Ben recited his list to Santa, and then it was 3-year-old Luke's turn. He climbed up on his mom's lap, and she said: 'Ho-ho-ho! What is your name, little boy?'

" 'My name is Luke,' he replied.

" 'And how old are you, Luke?' said Santa.

" 'I'm 41,' answered Luke."

Mother Earth of Eagan, at Christmastime: "Sometimes around this time of the year, I feel a little left out—because I'm Jewish.

"We were at an art show today, and my littlest boy was looking at the Nativity scene, and his face got so bright. And he goes: 'Mommy! Mommy, look! There's baby Moses!'

"I just thought it was so cute."

J.B. of the East Side: "We were watching my 8-year-old son do his Christmas show at church, and my 3-year-old was listening—and all of a sudden, he looks at me and he goes: 'Mom, what was *that*?'

"I said: 'I don't know. What do you mean?'

"And he goes: 'I heard crying.'

"You know, there's *lots* of kids crying and making noise and people talking and stuff, so I didn't really pay any attention to him.

"And he said: 'Mom!' His eyes got really big. 'I think it was baby Jesus!' "

Chris of the East Side: "About 20 years ago, when our son was about 5, we were shopping for a Christmas tree. We'd been to two different places, and my husband and I were bickering; couldn't find a tree we liked, and so we were arguing back and forth.

"Our son is looking at us, kind of crestfallen, and he says: 'Why do we have to go to another tree lot? What's wrong with the trees here?'

"And one of us said: 'Well, they aren't any good. We have to go find something else.'

"And he said: 'But they *all* look good to me!'

"We bought the next tree we saw, and we've never fought over what Christmas trees look like since—and we've had great trees."

Caitlin's Mom of Rosemount: "My husband and I took our daughter, who's 2½, shopping for Toys for Tots. On the way to the store, we explained that she could pick out the toys, but that she couldn't keep them; we told her that Santa would pick them up and deliver them to kids who weren't as lucky as she was and maybe didn't have a nice house to live in with lots of toys to play with.

"After this explanation, I asked her: 'So, honey, what do you want to buy the kids?'

"She looked at me and told me: 'A house.'

"Thinking she meant a dollhouse, I told her: 'A dollhouse sounds really nice.'

" 'No!' she replied. 'A *real* house for the poor kids who don't have one.'

"I explained that this was a very sweet idea, but Mommy really didn't have enough money to buy a real house for someone else.

"She told me: 'That's OK. Daddy can take the money out of the cash machine!'

"Later, after we bought the Toys for Tots, I told her that she could pick out one toy and I'd buy it for her.

"She told me: 'Let's buy another one for the poor kids, instead.'

"So we did.

"She was thrilled.

"Seems like this little 2½-year-old maybe understands Christmas better than some adults.

"Merry Christmas, everyone."

Kelly's Dad of Woodbury: "My daughter was working on her Christmas list last night. She's 6 years old and can spell a lot of words phonetically, but needs help with the bigger ones.

"Midway through her list, she asked me: 'How do you spell "everything"?'

"I thought to myself: 'Oh, no. What kind of a list is this going to be?'

"When she finished it, she showed it to me—and I'd like to read you the beginning:

" 'Daer Santa

" 'This is my things

" 'You dot have to bring everything

" 'But I want the doll that you do the hair'

"I guess she did find an unselfish way of fitting in the word 'everything.'"

Chief V of St. Paul: "My husband's niece got My Size Barbie from her papa for Christmas, on Christmas Eve. When it came time to go to bed that night, she placed Barbie near the table where she had left punch and cookies for Santa.

"She said: 'I'm going to leave Barbie here just in case Santa brings another one for me. That way, he can see I already got one, and he can give that one to another little girl that didn't get one.'

"I was touched, to say the least, by her unselfishness."

Mame of St. Paul: "My little nephew Matthew is 7, and he's not real sure about this Santa Claus stuff. He's just at that age.

"Last week, he asked me if I believed in Santa Claus, and I said: 'Well, yeah! I do!'

"And he said: 'I don't. Well, not *too* much.'"

Grandpa Ray of St. Paul: "Our granddaughter, who is now 6 years old, had just about made her final decision that the Santa Claus business wasn't what it was cracked up to be. When her mom and dad said that they would be taking her to visit Santa, our granddaughter—rather doubtful—said: 'Well, OK. We'll go.'

"Her dad maneuvered her up to the jolly old gent—and through his magic, Santa Claus called her by name

" 'Well, Shannon!' he exclaimed. 'Shannon, I'm sorry, but we have a problem'—and of course Shannon's ears stood right straight up, immediately, and her interest was fanned. 'Did you have a treat for me last year? Did you leave one out?'

" 'Yes,' Shannon said. 'I left cookies!'

" 'Well, did you just leave one? Or did you leave more than one?'

" 'Well, I left a whole bunch! And I left milk, too!' Shannon says.

" 'Well, Shannon, there was only one left—and no milk. You know that chair your dad always sits in? There were crumbs all over it.'

"Shannon turned around, glared at her father and said: 'Dad!'

"Poor Dad melted.

"She turned back to Santa and said: 'Don't you worry about a thing.'

"Faith renewed."

Cici of Rochester: "For the past five years, I've tried hard to be honest with my children—and patient. I've also tried to do all the '90s things, as far as behavior modification.

"But Sunday, the children—who are 4 and 5—were acting like little beasts. Finally, after exhausting all of my resources, I resorted to: 'Santa's watching. You'd better behave.'

"My Christopher told me: 'There's no such thing as Santa.'

"I was just devastated. He'd obviously thought about it—but wasn't totally convinced, because after an hour, he came up to me and asked: 'How can Santa possibly watch us all the time?'

"And I said, without missing a beat: 'The Christmas tree is a transmitter to the North Pole. That's how he knows.'

"It worked! Just before bed, Christopher and Andrew were under the tree, chatting up a storm."

H. of T. of Minneapolis: "Our 6-year-old daughter wanted desperately to believe in Santa Claus, although I know the skeptics at school were influencing her.

"One of the gifts she received from Santa was a snow globe with the 'Wizard of Oz' characters in it. She was studying it the other night before bed, and she said: 'Mom, I wasn't sure before whether Santa Claus was real and brought us stuff, but I've been lookin' *very closely* inside this snow globe, and I can tell that it was hand-painted by elves.'

"I thought that was the sweetest thing. I smile to myself every time I think of it."

Jerry of West St. Paul: "When my oldest boy was about 6 or 7, he came up to me one day and said: 'Dad, there really is no Santa Claus, is there?'

"I was pretty upset, thinking it was too early for him to start not believing. I said: 'Well, David, if there is no Santa Claus, who do you think brings the toys every Christmas?'

"He looked puzzled for a minute; he pondered, and he looked at me, and he said: 'The Easter bunny'—in all seriousness.

"Right then, I knew that we were still safe for a while. He kept on believing."

Glen of St. Paul: "When my brother Marvin was a toddler, which was 60-some years ago—he's 69 years young today—my father played Santa Claus. When he was through playing Santa, my father changed and came back where my brother was. He asked: 'Has Santa been here?'

"Marvin said: 'Yes—and he had shoes just like yours.'"

Sandy of Lakeland: "It's getting toward the time of year when I'm reminded of what my son did many years ago, when he was in kindergarten.

"I was paying some bills or something, and he came home from school, and he sat down at the table across from me. And he finally said: 'Mom?'

"And I said: 'Yes.'

"And he said: 'The kids at school said you're the Easter bunny.'

"And I sat there, and I said: 'Yeah. They're right.'

"He sat there; he didn't say anything at all for the longest time. But he just kept staring at me, and finally he opened up and said: 'Mom, don't you get tired going to all those houses?'"

Greasy Cece: "I attended the live Nativity pageant at the Hennepin Avenue United Methodist Church. It was a wonderful Christmas experience: The production was magnificent; the staging and costumes were beautiful; the cast of hundreds was so impressive. And the emphasis was right where it should be: on the beauty and simplicity of the story of the first Christmas.

"Then my 7-year-old nephew, Bub, turned it into a cute kid story. We were watching the procession of the Three Kings and their entourage: dozens of glittery people, most of them carrying treasure chests.

"Bub leaned over and said to me: 'Look at all those presents. Wow! They sure know how to give *him* a merry Christmas.'"

Christina of White Bear Township: "It was Good Friday, and my sister asked my mom: 'What was Good Friday all about? What happened then?' And my mom told her—went through the whole thing. Talked about: 'That's when Jesus died on the cross.'

"And when she got to the end, my sister screwed up her face, started crying, said: 'Ohhhhhh, then he missed Easter!'"

Scott of Columbia Heights: "I was talking to my 3½-year-old son, trying to explain the meaning of Easter to him—about how Jesus died and came back to life and went to heaven and was with God and all the other people who died before us and went to heaven.

"He looked at me very solemnly and said: 'Yes, Jesus was killed on the cross.'

"And I said: 'Yes, that's very good. What else can you tell me about Jesus?'

"And he said: 'Well, some people took him down, and they took him to the hospital, and they gave him some aspirin, and he's all better now.'

"Very solemn, very honest, and very, very hilarious."

Don W. of St. Paul: "During Easter, me and a bunch of the fellas went out to help little kids find Easter eggs. We put Easter eggs in our pockets for the little little ones.

"I put down an egg for a little girl, tapped her on the shoulder; she went over and picked up the egg. Walked a little ways and looked around—and here she is, following me!

"So I says: 'Aren't you gonna look for Easter eggs?'

"She says: 'No. I'm waitin' for you to put down another one.'"

A.B. of St. Paul: "I asked my 4-year-old niece for romantic advice. I asked her who she liked better: my past boyfriend, or my current boyfriend.

"I realize that it was pretty sad that I was looking to a 4-year-old for advice.

"But she looked up at me with her big eyes and kinda thought about it, and she said: 'I like *you!*'

"And I thought: 'Damn! That should've been *my* answer.'"

Jeanne of St. Paul: "When the grandchildren were dropped off this week, Katie—the 3-year-old—looked at her mom and dad and said: 'Stay out as long as you want. Because you *need* time together.'"

S.L. of Woodbury: "I had a frustrating day at work, and I came home kinda crabby, and I sat down at the counter—where us and our kids were gonna have dinner.

"I kinda pushed my kids arm's-length away and said: 'I need space tonight. Move over.'

"And my daughter said: 'Why?'

"And I said: 'I don't know. Just because.'

"And my son looks at me and says: 'Are your buns getting bigger, Mom?'"

Glamour Girl of Stillwater: "As I was approaching my 39th birthday, I started to think that it might be a good idea to look into learning how to use some makeup—especially since my sister's wedding is coming up. So I sat for 1½ hours at the Clinique counter to start my education.

"When I returned home, my family approved of my new look, but my 8-year-old daughter did ask me later, privately, if it hurt when they took all of those red lumps off my face."

Michelle of Cottage Grove: "I have a 2-year-old who has lately been taking my face in her hands and looking right into my eyes and saying, in this soft, whispery, just-so-sincere voice: 'You're *so* beautiful. You're just *so* beautiful.'

"I was feeling very tickled about that and very proud—until today, on 'Mike & Maty,' they brought out this giant iguana, and she looked at the TV and said: 'Oh, that's *so* beautiful. That's *so* beautiful.'"

Jim of St. Paul: "My son has a pet iguana, and he took it to school to show some of the other kids. If you've ever seen an iguana, they have a large flap of skin that hangs down from their neck, and it's called a dewlap.

"The kids were asking what it was, and he explained, and a little girl in his class said: 'Oh! My grandma has one of those.'"

Gayle of Isanti: "My daughter, Amy, who is 7 years old, has always loved the feel of my mom's (face) cheeks. *[Bulletin Board notes: Thanks for the clarification, Gayle.]* 'Sooooo soft,' she says.

"Last summer, Grandma sat with the kids while I attended my class reunion. At one point, Amy snuggled up on the couch next to Grandma and, touching her cheek, asked: 'Grandma, were you pretty when you were young?'

"Mom was still laughing when I got home."

Karen S. of South St. Paul: "My granddaughter was about 6 years old, and she was at my house, and we were getting ready to go to a family reunion.

"I told her: 'Lauren, you go in and take a bath now, and then, while you're doing your hair and things, Grandma's gonna go in and take her shower.'

"And she said: 'But Grandma, I want to take a shower with *you!*'

"And I said: 'No, Lauren, Grandma just wants to take a shower all by herself.'

"She said: 'Come on, Grandma. *Please* let me take a shower with you.'

"And I said: 'No, Lauren. Grandma's gonna take her shower alone.'

"She looked at me, and she said: 'Oh, come on, Grandma. I won't laugh. I promise.'

"How deflating."

Lute of Fisk Street: "My daughter was explaining to her grandma that we're gonna have a new arrival at our house—and what she said was, unfortunately: 'Grandma, when Mom's tummy gets to be as big as yours, she's gonna have a baby.'

"Fortunately, Grandma has a sense of humor."

Gretchen of St. Paul: "Last night, we were at my sister's house for her birthday. We were all sitting around the table eating when my father suddenly stood up and set his plate down and said: 'That's enough food for Grandpa. I don't want to get fat.'

"My sister's 5-year-old got a funny look on her face and said: 'That's OK, Grandpa. You're already fat.'

"I guess he must have taken into account what she said, because he didn't skip the hot-fudge sundae we had for dessert."

Laraine of Cottage Grove: "My 4-year-old grandson asked me about the wrinkles in my forehead: 'Grandma, did you stay in the bathtub too long?'"

Helen of St. Paul Park: "My son died last summer, and his wife just sold the house. She called me one night to tell me about the new people who would be my neighbors; she wanted to know if I'd like to meet the new tenants. Of course I was tickled to go over and meet them.

"They were a young couple with two young kids; the baby was about a year old, and the older one was 4. When they came, I said: 'Why don't you go through the house? Take your time, and I'll take the little kids, so you won't have to bother with them.'

"The 4-year-old turned out to be a real smart little gal. The first thing she does is pick up a little flower and gave it to me and said: 'Are you allergic? 'Cause if you're allergic, you *must not* smell that flower.' But anyway, we walked around, and pretty soon I said: 'Let's sit down. I'm tired. Let's sit down and just talk.'

"She sat down beside me, and she started staring at my face. And she looked and she looked, and finally she said: 'You got cracks in your face! What ever happened?' I really think that's cute. When you get to be 86, you have a lot of wrinkles. I told her mother about it, and she said that I was probably the first old person that she'd ever gotten close to."

Marge of Little Canada: "I was giving my 3½-year-old grand-daughter a bath the other day.

"When we were done, I was drying her off. She was sitting on my lap, and she got real close to my face, and she looked at me and started running her finger across my face, and she said: 'Oh, my God, Grandma! Your face is cracked!'"

Marian and Judy of West St. Paul, who were told this story by their friend LaVonne: "LaVonne had surgery on her feet and was home recuperating. Her family was there visiting her, and they were all looking at old photographs.

"They came across LaVonne's high-school graduation picture. One of the grandchildren, age 3, asked who that was and was told it was Grandma. She looked at the picture, looking at her grandmother, patted her arm and said, 'Grandma, maybe when your feet get better, your face will get better, too.'"

Deb of Shoreview: "My mother, who has reached the age of senior-citizen discounts, keeps a box of that expensive facial soap in the green-plastic box by her bathroom sink.

"My 7-year-old nephew saw the box and asked her what it was for.

"Grandma said: 'I use a special soap on my face so that I don't get wrinkles.'

"Ted looked at her closely for a few minutes and then said: 'Grandma, I don't think it's working.'"

Chuckles of St. Paul: "While I was visiting some friends in Texas, somehow our topic of conversation wound up being how I am follicularly challenged.

"My friends' 10-year-old daughter noted that I have some hair on the top—and asked me when was the last time I had it cut. I told her that it was probably close to 20 years, but that I wouldn't let a barber touch it 'cause I'm trying to get it to grow back.

"She got this grimace on her face and said: 'Well, I hate to tell you this, but you're not making very good progress.'"

Al L. of St. Paul: "I was cutting my grandson's hair yesterday, and he asked me: 'Grandpa, where do you find a barber that cuts your hair? He leaves so much on the sides and cuts it all off on top!'"

Jean of St. Paul: "When our granddaughter was about 3, she decided to play Doctor with her grandpa. She used the tiny little flashlight, and she examined each ear very carefully, each eye, his mouth and teeth.

"Then she looked in his nose, and she disgustedly quit, with the remark: 'I can't see a thing with all that fur.'"

Kirsten of St. Paul: "This morning, my almost completely bald father-in-law was talking to my 3-year-old daughter, Hannah.

"He said: 'If I had hair, I'd want it to be curly—like yours.'

"Then Hannah said: 'Although, Papa, that white stuff *kind of* looks like hair.'"

Jerry of St. Paul: "Our grandson Zach, who always calls me 'Papa,' was sitting across the table from me as we were eating dinner.

"Out of the clear blue, he looked at me and said: 'Papa, you don't have any hair.'

"I laughed and agreed with him. I then told him that someday he would be just like me.

"He lifted up his thumbs in a gesture of approval and responded with 'Cool!'

"What a kid."

Malone's Mentor: "My nephew Matthew is still at that age where he will actually give me a big hug when I ask for one. (Sometimes I don't even have to ask!)

"A couple of weeks ago, he gave me a big I Love You hug, When I was holding him in my arms, I asked Matt what I am going to do when he gets too big for me to hold.

"He put his sweet little head on my shoulder and said: 'I'll hold you.'

"What a guy."

Grandma T. of Wyoming: "My 4-year-old granddaughter was holding a hair barrette that was curved and colored like a rainbow, and she said: 'You know, Grandma, there's a pot of gold at the end of the rainbow.'

"I answered: 'I know, and I wish I had a little of that gold right now.'

"And she responded: 'Oh, but you have, Grandma! Me!'

"And, you know, she was right—and I have five more little grandchildren to increase that gold."

Jeanne of St. Paul: "My 91-year-old neighbor told me this story:

"Many years ago, she was visiting her daughter and son-in-law and granddaughter, and she had stayed a few days. She said to the granddaughter: 'Grandma's going home tomorrow.'

"And there was just silence, and then the little granddaughter said: 'Well, you've stayed long enough.'

"There was a silence again, and then she said: 'Now, when you go home, we can visit *you*.'"

Rhonda of Woodbury: "My 1½-year-old daughter is learning how to talk, and we were helping her practice.

"I said: 'Can you say "Mommy"?'

"And she said: 'Mommy.'

"And I said: 'Can you say "Daddy"?'

"And she said: 'Daddy.'

"And Grandpa said: 'Who am I?'

"She gave him a big smile and said: 'Mine.'"

Diana of Lake Elmo: "When our oldest son, Nick, was 3, Grandpa Bernie was lying on his bed and Nick was playing Doctor—wearing a stethoscope, doctor pajamas, and a pair of old sunglasses. He had his doctor kit open on the bed.

"He looked in Grandpa's ears and listened to his lungs and heart and made him open his mouth.

"Grandpa asked: 'Doctor, what's wrong with me? My heart goes pitter-patter, patter-pitter?'

"Nick took off his glasses and said: 'Bernie, I think you have a broken testicle bone.'"

Uncle Jed of Winona: "My 7-year-old niece, Lindsey, was playing Doctor with her 3-year-old sister, Megan.

"After checking her over, Lindsey proclaimed: 'Meggie, you've got intestines in your head.'

"Her mother overheard this and informed her that people don't have intestines in their head.

"Lindsey replied: 'I know. That's what's wrong with her.'"

Susan's Husband of Bloomington, Ill.: "My 10-year-old son just informed us that if you're ever swimming and a shark comes near, you should stand perfectly still.

"My wife pointed out that you'd sink straight to the bottom.

" 'Yeah, I know,' he said. 'That's one problem.' "

Susan of North St. Paul: "When I lived in Brainerd, some of my favorite people were Deb and Ray and their children, Andy and Alyssa.

"When Andy was just 5 years old, he asked me to play the kids' version of Trivial Pursuit. Well, I should have known better than to accept, since Andy's been simply brilliant since day one.

"My question, from the Nursery Rhymes category, was: 'In "Baby Bunting," what does Daddy go hunting for?'

"Smugly, I answered: 'Well, that's easy. A rabbit skin.'

"Andy gave me credit, but added: 'Actually, you hunt for rabbit. The skin comes along with it.' "

Anne of the Midway: "When my brother was about 10, he had a rabbit, and one day my mother looked out the back window to see him out by the hutch. She went out to find him holding a dead rabbit.

"With tears in his eyes, he said, '*Everybody* dies! First Hubert Humphrey, then the Pope, now my bunny.' "

The Arlington Panther of St. Paul: "Last week in church, during prayer request, a young lad about 5 years old stated to the pastor that his bunny had died, and he wanted to pray for it. The pastor said to the young lad that he would certainly pray for him to find comfort during this time of sorrow—to which the young lad responded: 'Oh, no. I just want a new bunny.' "

Young **Mink Lake** of Roseville: "I have a *really* cute kid story: I was baby-sitting for this girl, and I had to, like, watch her, because she was the flower girl in a wedding, and then I had to take her home and baby-sit for her.

"She was all dressed up in her little white flower-girl dress, and she had to walk down the aisle and, you know, throw the little rose petals on the ground.

"She's this really neat little girl; she's, like, I don't know, I think 3?

"And she walked down, and she took 'em out one by one and, like, bent over and put 'em on the aisle.

"And it was really, really cute."

Barbara of Andover: "I have a cute kid story; at least I think it's cute. It's about a little friend of mine, whose name was Vanessa.

"A couple of years ago, when she was 5, a friend of hers gave her a shedded snakeskin, and she was going to take it to school for show-and-tell. She had it in a Band-Aid box, and she was practicing all day to play a trick on her dad. When he came home, she was going to say: 'Oh, Dad! Do you want a Band-Aid?' He was going to open it and get the surprise of his life.

"So she's practicing and practicing on me, and her dad finally came home, and she said: 'Oh, Dad!'—and held it up to him and said: 'You want a snake?' So the joke didn't work.

"A footnote to this story is that Vanessa did die this April, at the age of 7, of kidney and liver failure. I miss her a lot. I think about her a lot. She had a lot of cute kid stories."

Joy of Vadnais Heights: "I was watching my grandchildren after school yesterday. It was raining, so I let Ben, who's 7, invite his friend Mike over to play. Well, Ben's brother Sam, who's 5, thought this was great; he thought they were going to play with him, too, so he followed 'em all over.

"After about 10 minutes of trying to lose Sam, Ben turned to him and said: 'You're such a pest! Why do you keep following us around?'

"Sam says: ' 'Cause I *love* you guys.'

"Well, Ben and Mike thought a minute, and then looked at each other, and then looked at Sam and said: 'Oh, all right. Come on.' And they played nice until the sun came out.

"I call this Innocent Wisdom. It's always about love, and it always works."

Linda of Hastings: "I'm a mother of three boys, and just when I think I know them pretty well, one of them will do something to amaze me. Yesterday, it happened again.

"My middle son, Nick, is a fifth-grader. His school has a great program called Banking on Behavior. Each week, the kids earn a 'salary,' which is recorded in their checkbooks. From that income, they must pay rent for their desks, along with other miscellaneous expenses. Each day, they can earn bonuses for good behavior, but are expected to pay 'fines' for bad behavior or late assignments.

"At the end of each quarter, they hold a big auction where the students can spend their money on items donated by parents and local businesses.

"Nick took this program very seriously, worked very hard and was able to save over $1,000 in anticipation of this auction. Yesterday after the auction, Nick came home from school with his prize carefully hidden in a brown paper bag.

"This is the amazing part: He had spent all of his money on a birthday present for his older brother, T.J., and bought nothing for himself.

"What a great kid."

Pooter of St. Paul: "My 9-year-old son, Charlie, has a best friend, Lori; they are inseparable.

"This summer, when Charlie pulled his bike out of the basement, he realized that he really couldn't utilize it to its fullest potential because Lori didn't have a bike. So he started saving the spending-money portion of his allowance, and after a month, we went garage-saleing and found Lori a bike.

"He talked the seller down from $15 to $10, and we loaded it up, took it home, adjusted it and presented it to Lori.

"I had to tell Lori that it was a gift from Charlie from his own allowance, because Charlie didn't say anything. Now I know it was because *that* wasn't the important point. The important thing was that Lori now had a bike, and they were free!

"They zoomed around the neighborhood; they played chase games, spy games—and had a glorious time. Charlie expressed his love of freedom and escape and said that they felt like airplanes flying around—for three days . . . until Lori left her bike outside and it was stolen.

"When she told Charlie, he didn't say much. While he was out riding, alone, we were talking about it—in an adult fashion: 'How could she be so inconsiderate? So irresponsible! Charlie worked hard for that money! Ten bucks—down the drain. Try and do something nice for people, and see what happens'—*et cetera*. This was two adults talking.

"When Charlie got home, I asked him how *he* felt about Lori's bike being stolen. I was ready to commiserate with him; you know: 'It's the thought that counts. Some people aren't very responsible, but I'm sure she meant no insult to your generosity.' I was just waiting for him to express his anger or disappointment.

"Well, he paused for a minute and then said: 'It's just really sad, because now she can't get away from the house.' Geez. *His* generosity and empathy and caring and unselfish love caught me with my emotional pants down. It was a beautiful and eye-opening moment.

"I will be *happy* to put my old age in the hands of such wonderful kids.

"And to top this story off: Lori's parents realized how wonderful these two are together—and got her a bike right away. So the two of them are off in the neighborhood, spreading goodwill and true friendship wherever they go.

"Thanks, kids."

Lori of Woodbury: "My sister and I were sitting outside, talking. We had our kids out there playing, and these two boys come riding down the street. They must've been, oh, 9 or 10—and at that age, when kids start yelling at each other, usually you hear profanity.

"Well, this one little boy got just irate. He was very upset with his other friend. He looked back at him, on his bike, and he yelled: 'You know, you're just a little . . .'—and I thought for sure he was gonna start to swear, and it was the cutest thing: He says, 'You're just a little . . . urchin.'

"My sister and I laughed so hard."

L. F-A. of Mahtomedi: "When my daughter Carrie was 3 years old, she got her first trike. We live on a dead end, so riding in the street was not too dangerous, but her dad painted a line across the street and told her not to drive over that line.

"He really drilled this into her, and we felt pretty confident that she understood—until we saw her ride up to the line, get off her trike, carry the trike over the line, get back on and continue merrily down the street."

Rita of Shoreview: "Our 4-year-old daughter has just recently figured out how to ride her bike without the training wheels, and she learned how to blow a bubble with real bubble gum, and she even got her ears pierced the other day and didn't even cry. So her dad and I are totally overwhelmed by this rate of independence. *[BULLETIN BOARD INTERRUPTS: We're totally overwhelmed— not to say appalled—by the picture of a 4-year-old girl getting her ears pierced. Yikes!]*

"We were driving last night, and she decided she knew her right hand from her left hand. She just announced: 'Mom, this is my right hand'—and she was right. My husband and I looked at each other, and we were so pleased and so proud; you could see us just beaming at each other.

" 'Yep,' she said, 'this is my right hand, and nobody *told* me.'

"And then she said: 'This is my other right hand'—and she pointed to her left hand. We kind of deflated ourselves and went on driving."

Susan of North St. Paul: "I sent my 4-year-old daughter, Liddee, to her room to pick up—under threat of no TV, no candy until she did. Fifteen minutes later, she burst into the living room, jubilantly crying: 'Mom! Mom! You should see my room! It's as clean as a pig sty!'

"And, of course, it was."

A Grandma of Eagan: "My daughter Ann was on vacation in France. She'd made arrangements with a florist to bring flowers for my birthday. I was on the phone talking to my 7-year-old grand-daughter, Amber, and told her that Ann had sent me flowers and a man had delivered them to the door.

"Amber said: 'Did he speak French?'

"Sweet innocence."

Barb of Eagan: "I had bought a new pair of boots for my 5-year-old daughter, and she decided that the box was just the perfect size to put all of her little treasures in. She took it around the house and loaded it with all of her special things.

"And then she was concerned that maybe a burglar would come

to our house and find her box, so she sat down and thought about it—and asked me, then, how to spell 'empty box.'

"She wrote 'EMPTY BOX' on the top of it.

"If burglars come, there's no way they'll look into it now."

Debby of Cottage Grove: "I have a son, a second-grader, who gets himself ready pretty independently in the morning. But we had a problem last week: After he had left to go to school, I went into the upstairs bathroom, where he chooses to get ready, and I found his underwear from the day before behind the bathroom door.

"All week long, not even thinking about it, I picked them up and went into his room and threw them down the chute—until Friday came, and I felt much like his maid, and I proceeded to tell him when he got home that we needed to work on this problem. He said he would work on it. I told him that it was very unfair—and that if I had a dime for every pair of underwear of his that I threw down the chute, I would be rich.

"So come Monday morning, I was up in the bathroom and I happened to glance that way, and sure enough, there was his pair of underwear behind the door—only on Monday, they had a dime on top of them."

Mary Conroy of Plymouth: "About five years ago, I asked our son Joey, who was 4 at the time, if he had changed his underwear lately, because I hadn't seen any in the dirty-laundry basket for a while. He assured me that he got a clean pair on every day.

"Still not sure he was telling the truth, I told him to get in the bathtub. Off comes the shirt, off come the socks, off come the shorts—and, sure enough, six layers of underwear."

D.C. of St. Paul: "I've gotta tell you about this trip up north we took yesterday, my wife and I.

"We left St. Paul at 6 o'clock in the morning and drove for about an hour, and then we stopped for breakfast up at Perkins. After we had breakfast, on the way out, I went into the head. A young fellow came in after me with his young son, who was all bundled up because it was very cold.

"The son immediately went into the biffy that had a door on it, and after a short time, the lad started to groan a little. His father said: 'Nicholas, what's the problem?' There was no answer, but another little groan—and again: 'Nicholas, what's your *problem?*'

"Again there was no answer, but the kid groaned a little bit, and the father said: 'Nicholas . . . '—but he couldn't get any further than that when the kid came back and says: 'I can't *find* it to take it out!' "

Beth of White Bear Lake: "Our family had spaghetti with meatballs for dinner last night. The kids don't really like meatballs, and our 3-year-old daughter, Rachel, *really* didn't want to eat her meatballs—but, of course, she had to, because they were on her plate, and she has to eat everything on her plate.

"Anyhow, before she went to bed, she was trying to go to the potty, and we put her on the toilet, and she said: 'I tried and I tried and I tried, Mom, but I just can't. I must have a meatball stuck in my butt.' "

L.R. of Barron, Wis.: "The other day, I was picking my 3-month-old son up from the baby-sitter's house, and another one of the mothers was picking up her 5-year-old son and 2-year-old daughter.

"As they were getting ready to leave, the little girl was trying to adjust her underwear to a more comfortable position, and the mother said: 'What's wrong? Are your undies in a bundle?'

"The little girl looked at her with a puzzled look on her face and said: 'No, Mom, they're in my butt.'

"Had to laugh."

Lee of Apple Valley: "Two-year-old Phillip is in the process of toilet-training. Every time he performs, he is rewarded with three M&Ms.

"One day, while sitting on his potty chair, unable to perform, he said: 'I guess I'm just not hungry yet.' "

The Dartman of Dinkytown: "My sister has a toddler who's just beginning to learn proper bathroom habits—and apparently my sister lets Abigail follow her into the bathroom and see how things are done.

"The other day, Abigail ran into the bathroom, pushed down her diaper and sat on her little potty trainer. Then she looked at my sister and said: 'Need book.'"

Mike and Geri of Maplewood: "We were getting Andy ready for a bath. He was standing naked, ready to get into the bathtub, when he suddenly decided he had to go to the bathroom first.

"Standing at the toilet, he turned and said: 'You know, every time It sees a toilet, It just has to go.'"

Mary Ann of Apple Valley, speaking of her 4-year-old daughter: "When we were visiting her grandparents this past week, Grandma gave her a candy cane, and she couldn't understand why she couldn't eat this candy cane 'til after breakfast.

"She said: 'You know, it's not me that wants to eat the candy cane; it's the candy cane that wants me to eat it.'"

Pam of Stillwater: "When our son was about 4 years old, we took him fishing. We kept telling him: 'Honey, now you've gotta watch your bobber, because when the bobber goes under, that means there's a fish there.' We kept saying: 'Gotta watch your bobber. Gotta watch your bobber—'cause if it goes under, that means there's a fish there.'

"After about four or five times, he looked up at me and said: 'Mom, how does the bobber know when a fish is there?'"

Gene of New Brighton: "I was downstairs working in my workshop, and my little granddaughter, who's about 4 years old, was down there pedaling away for all she's worth on one of these exercise bikes; it was set for about zero pressure.

"She came over to me, and she says: 'Grandpa, I almost got to the 2 and zero.'

"And I said: 'You keep tryin', and you'll get there.'

"She stepped back and looked at me. She says: 'I can't.'

"And I says: 'Why can't you?'

"And she said: 'Because these shoes won't go that fast.'

"And then: 'Grandpa, why are you laughing?'"

Lori of Woodbury: "We have two children: Matthew, 5, and Lillie, 4. And as mothers are apt to do, I'm very frequently commenting to these growing kids that their shoes—or other items of clothing—are getting too small.

"When I made this comment for the umpteenth time yesterday, Matt said to me: 'Mom, how do shoes shrink?'

"I just love it. They always give me a new way to look at life."

Ruthe of Mendota Heights: "Many years ago, when our oldest daughter was about 4 years old, she got new black patent-leather shoes for Easter. These were not easy to come by in the '50s.

"She was limping around, and I said to her: 'Honey, do your new shoes hurt?'

"And she replied: 'Oh, no, Mommy. The shoes feel fine. It's just my feet that hurt.'"

The Commissioner of Tracy: "The recent warm weather reminds me of the way my youngest son, Jordan, first asked to go barefoot: 'Can I wear my toes outside?'"

Deb of Lino Lakes: "When my daughter was 3 years old, she came to me and told me she was hungry. I wanted to finish what I was doing before I made her something to eat. To buy myself a few more minutes, I told her to go into the kitchen and take a bite of Dad's toast.

"Following my instructions, she went into the kitchen, crawled under the table and bit her dad's toe."

BULLETIN BOARD MUSES: And Deb's daughter hasn't trusted her since.

A Mom of the Midway: "I'm calling about my 4-year-old, who will be 5 on Sunday. Her name is Claire.

"She has a unique—maybe it's not unique to 4-year-olds, but it seems unique to adults, anyway—sense of logic. And because she's having a birthday and I'm thinking about her growing up and getting bigger—it's one of the things I'm going to miss as she does that. Anyway, here's an example:

"We were looking for her slip-on shoes, because I was so tired of helping her tie her shoes every time she came in the house, which was every two minutes. So I said: 'Come upstairs, and let's find your slip-ons. You look under the bed while I look in this pile of stuff over here.'

"So she looks under the bed, and she says: 'Mom, kitty's under here.'

"I said: 'That's nice. Find your shoes, please.'

"And in a minute, she says: 'I've got kitty!'

"And I looked, and I said: 'Well, you're not supposed to be finding the cat, Claire. You're supposed to be finding your shoes.'

"And she looked at me and said: 'But *Mom!* Cats don't *wear* shoes.'

"And who can argue with that?"

BULLETIN BOARD TESTIFIES, FROM VERY RECENT EXPE-RIENCE OF A 4-YEAR-OLD GIRL: Just wait 'til she ties her own shoes for the first time. You'll never have seen a better smile in your life, and you'll think: "Man, is it a gas to have a 5-year-old!"

The Woman in the Shoe of Andover: "One day, our cat must have had a hairball, because she was honking and hacking for a good part of the day.

"About a week or so later, as I was making breakfast, I heard this honking and hacking—and it was my 3-year-old, with a croupy cough.

"She came downstairs and said: 'Mom, I caught a cold from kitty.'

"I thought that was pretty cute."

Gypsi of New Brighton: "I'm calling about my beautiful little girls, Al Pal and Chy-Chy.

"This last week, we weren't feeling very well; we were getting over colds, and my niece and nephew, Louise and Seth—ages 8 and 13—came to stay with us for five days.

"They brought some Berry Berry Kix along—which, of course, is one of my favorites, so I happened to share them . . . and basically finish the box. So I told them that I was going to get them the next time I went to the grocery store.

"After I came home from the grocery store, I sat down to have me a nice big bowl of Berry Berry Kix, and Chy-Chy—who's 18 months—came to sit on my lap and share some of my Berry Berry

Kix. She started eating them with her hands and stuffing them into her mouth, which she tends to do—and as I set her down to go put my bowl in the sink, I noticed that she was choking, starting to gag.

"It's a very scary story at this point; I'm not sure if she's choking or gagging; I pick her up and give her a brief little Heimlich, just enough to get her to push it out; pick her up and carry her over to the sink . . . but she manages to leave a trail of vomit all the way to the sink.

"I'm comforting her, and she's a little upset—and in comes Al Pal to say: 'Oh, nooooo. Chy-Chy throw up?' And she looks at the floor and turns to my niece, Louise, and says: 'Hey, Mom bought more Berry Berry Kix!' "

Monkey Woman of Eagan: "My sister was on vacation, so my husband and my 3-year-old son, Alec, went to her house to feed her cats. A couple minutes after the dry cat food was poured, Alec went into the kitchen and started yelling: 'Hey, Dad, the cats are eating oatmeal!'

"So Dad went to check it out—and the cat had vomited and was reconsuming it.

"Alec kept asking: 'How did the cat get the oatmeal?' "

L. Brown of Mendota Heights: "When our daughter was 3 or 4, we got a kitten. When our daughter saw him washing, she said: 'Look, Mom! He's tasting his arms!' "

Nancy of Lakeville: "When my daughter was about 3, my father took us out to dinner at Chi-Chi's, and I ordered her a Kiddie Cocktail—a non-alcoholic cocktail. Strawberry. She peered into the glass at that frothy red drink, and she said: 'Are there *kitties* in here?' "

R.J.'s Mom: "My son is 5, and the other day, he had found this can of tennis balls in the garage, and he took 'em downstairs to play.

"He was playing with the dog, and the dog was pickin' up the balls with his mouth and bringin' 'em back to R.J., playing fetch and drooling, and my son came upstairs after about 15 minutes, and he was very angry.

"I said: 'What's the matter?'

"And he looked at me with this mad little look on his face, and he held up this tennis ball covered with spit, and he says to me: 'Look at what that dog did, Mom. That's the last time I let *him* chew on my balls.'

"I loved it."

Ellen of St. Paul: "When my son was 3, I invited him to sit on my lap in a chair, to read a story to him. He said no—and to come sit with him on the floor, because it would be more fun. So I consented and sat down on the floor, and he sat on my lap.

"As I started the book, he arched his back in the way that kids always do and whapped me on the tender part of my nose with his hard little head. I immediately started to bleed from my nose and pushed him off my lap—and I'm trying to stanch the flow of blood and not moan too loudly in pain when the dog sees me and decides to take advantage of the situation by mobbing me and doing the other things that male dogs will do when they're overly excited.

"So I'm stanching the flow of blood with one hand and beating the dog off with the other. *[BULLETIN BOARD NOTES: Oh, dear! This is getting complicated.]* I finally get the dog settled down, and my son looks at me with perfectly straight face and round eyes and says: 'See, Mom? I *told* you it'd be more fun down here on the floor.'"

Big Wally of White Bear: "My 6-year-old daughter, Ann, comes bouncing home from kindergarten the other day and runs in the house, all excited to tell me about her day. But our 1-year-old black Lab, Molly, just wouldn't leave her alone; she was starving for attention.

"So I says to her: 'Ann, why don't you just put your bag down and pet Molly for a little bit, and then she'll leave you alone and you can come and talk to me and show me your schoolwork.'

"So, while she's petting Molly, she says: 'Molly likes it when I scratch her ears, and when I scratch under her chin, and when I scratch her nose, and when I pet her on her tummy, and when I pet her on her back.'

"And I said: 'Ann, I think Molly just likes to have you pet her, period.'

"And she looks all around the dog for a minute, and then she asks me: 'Dad, where's her period?'"

Jeri of Shell Lake, Wis.: "Recently, we acquired a new puppy—but before we chose which type of dog we wanted, we wanted to choose its sex. Our daughter Kelsey, who is 6, insisted that we get a female dog this time.

"I said: 'Why do you want a female?'

"She said: 'So I can pet it farther down.' "

BULLETIN BOARD NOTES: You remember Kelsey! She's the girl whose canine dietary exploits were broadcast to the whole congregation.

Anonymous of Inver Grove Heights: "A couple of summers ago, our two boys caught a garter snake that they wanted to keep for a pet.

"When I asked the 5-year-old what he wanted to name it, he named it Smashy. And I asked him why, and he said: 'Then if he ever gets run over or gets smashed, we can still call him by his name.' "

Sandy of Lake Elmo: "One day a few years ago, when my son was about 4 years old, he saw an ad in the paper for a pet store, with aquariums and fish on sale. He said: 'Mommy, can we *please* get a fish? Please, please, please!'

"I said: 'No, Bobby. We have a dog, and one pet is enough until you're old enough to take care of them yourself.'

"And he replied: 'Well, when the dog gets hit by a car, *then* can we get a fish?'

"Can you believe it?"

Cherry of Eagan: "Several years ago, my kids found a stray cat during a rainstorm. Of course, we brought her in—and in due time, she presented us with four kittens.

"When the kittens were old enough, I put a sign in the front yard saying 'Free Kittens,' and that afternoon, a little guy came to the door and asked if he could come in and look at the kittens. I told him: 'Sure.'

"He came in, and he says: 'Can I have one?'

"I said: 'You go get a note from your mom saying you can have a kitten, and you can take one home.'

"So he went back home and got the note, came in, picked out his kitten.

"Next morning, little knock came on the door. I answer the door, and he says: 'I want to exchange my kitten.'

"I said: 'Well, what's the matter with this one? Don't you like it?'

"He says: 'It's really cute—but this one's got sharp feet.'"

Grandma of Cottage Grove: "This weekend, my young granddaughter was visiting her brand-new kitty. She can't keep it at their apartment, and until they move, I'm baby-sitting for her.

"As she was holding the kitty, she said: 'You know, kitty, you bite and you scratch—and if you weren't *my* kitty, I wouldn't like you very much.'

"That's sort of like what we feel about our own kids at times, hmmm?"

D.G. of Oakdale: "This past weekend, I rented a lawn aerator— and my neighbor did his lawn, also. That night, as we took our puppy on our evening walk, the neighbors' granddaughter came up to us and said: 'Your puppy pooped all over my grandpa's yard.'

"I told her that Fanny wouldn't do that and that her grandpa did that to his yard.

"This cute little girl said: 'Grandpa didn't do that. They're too small. That has to be a dog or a cat.'"

A Mom of the Midway: "My 5-year-old, Claire, was chasing the cat this morning—which the cat didn't really appreciate . . . and I didn't really appreciate, because she was supposed to be getting ready for school.

"I said: 'Claire, quit chasing the cat. She's never gonna like you if you don't quit that.'

"She said to me—Claire, not the cat: 'She'll like me when I'm 18.'

"And I said: 'Not if you don't quit chasing her, she won't.'

"She said: 'But I'll know better by then!'

"And the funny part is: When she says these things to me, she makes it sound like *I'm* the one who's being silly. She just gets this tone of voice like 'Mom! *C'mon!*'"

Jill of St. Paul: "I was visiting my brother in northern Wisconsin about a month ago, and I took my niece Sadie to a fair. When we

were driving home that night, it was pretty clear out, so I was pointing out the full moon and some stars, and I tried showing her where
the Big Dipper was, and she was having a problem seeing it, so I
told her I'd show it to her when we got home.

"She said: 'Oh, yeah—like it's gonna follow us home.'"

Gayle of St. Paul: "I was taking my daughter, 9 years old, to the
park one day, and I was turnin' around, and my tires shrieked.

"And she says: 'Oh, Ma, quit tryin' to show off.'

"And I said: 'No, my tires are bald.'

"And she goes: 'Yeah, right, Ma—like tires have *hair*.'"

Donna of Vancouver, B.C.: "When my two daughters were little,
they would follow me everywhere I went. When I went outside,
they'd follow behind. If I took a bath, they'd have their clothes off
and would climb in before I could stop them. One day, I wanted
some privacy in the bathroom, so I ran in quick and locked the
door. They followed me and started banging on the door, demand-
ing to be let in.

"I jokingly told them: 'Not by the hair of my chinny-chin-chin!'

"There was silence for about five seconds. Then the oldest one
demanded, 'Open up, pig.'"

The Pretzel Addict of South St. Paul: "I have a 2-year-old who
doesn't have a lot of respect for my privacy.

"I was in the bathroom one day, and the door comes crashin'
open, and he says to me: 'Whatcha doin', Mommy?'

"To which I said: 'I'm going potty—and I don't need your help.'

"He said: 'Fine. You can just do it yourself.'

"I guess he told *me*."

Jack's Mom of Burnsville: "Jack's almost 5, and he has discovered . . . opinions. (Where he gets this opinionated streak, I really
have no idea.) But we've had little chats about how people can agree
to disagree, how he can think one thing and I can think another and
one of us isn't necessarily wrong—because at least five times a day, I
hear: 'You're *wrong*, Mom!'

"Anyway, we were having this little chat about disagreement—

and he really caught on to the point, and we agreed to disagree about whatever it was, and he said: 'OK, Mom, I disagree—and you're *wrong,* Mom!'"

Wendee of Oak Park Heights: "We were in Spooner, Wisconsin, camping, and the weather was miserable, and my daughter was driving us crazy, so we loaded her up in the car and decided to head up to Duluth and see Gooseberry Falls and Split Rock Lighthouse and all the little sights up that way.

"She whined and cried the whole way up; she wanted to go back to the campground and play, and was bugging us, asking us a thousand questions. We got to Split Rock Lighthouse, and I had had enough. She asked me why we were there, and I said that we were spending . . . quality . . . family . . . time together. And that shut her up for a little while.

"About 10 minutes later, she pulled on my coat and very sweetly asked me: 'Mommy, when quality's all done, can we *please* go back to the campground?'"

Kathy of Blaine: "My little girl just turned 5. We were in the store, and I saw the new Crayola washable crayons. I was commenting out loud: 'Oh, there's the washable crayons. I've been wanting to try those.' She was really excited about it.

"We got home, and she was coloring, and I was doing some other things, and I turned around and she was standing there with the crayons, one in each hand, and she said: 'Do I use *hot* water, Mom, or cold water to wash these crayons?' *[Bulletin Board notes: At 5 years old, it is apparently still possible for a mind to remain so unpolluted with un-sense that words are expected to mean what they say. Bravo, little girl! Washable crayons, indeed.]*

"Once I explained it to her, she proceeded to write all over the counter top—and got a big charge out of the fact that I didn't get too upset about it, because they really did wash off. It was great."

Grandma Cricket of Mahtomedi: "Two of my little granddaughters were here this afternoon—Stephanie, who's 6, and Kasey Jo, who's 4. They were sitting at the coffee table, each with her own little pad of paper, coloring with markers, and little Kasey asked Stephanie to draw her a steering wheel.

"Stephanie's *very* precise with everything she does. She drew a picture of a perfect steering wheel, and she drew a gearshift coming out the side of it.

"Well, Kasey Jo wanted it cut out, so Stephanie got the scissors and carefully cut out the steering wheel and the gearshift and gave it back to Kasey Jo.

"Kasey said: 'I don't want this on here'—pointing to the gearshift.

"Stephanie explained to her why you couldn't drive a car without a gearshift; she didn't know why, but she said you had to push it up and down, and there was a place there where you had to put the key in to start the car, and you really needed the gearshift on there.

"Kasey argued back—and they went back and forth for about two or three minutes. Then it got very quiet, and in kind of a disgusted way, Kasey Jo said, with her little lisp: 'Stephanie, it's only paper. Cut it off!'

"Aren't kids great?"

R.C. of Linden Hills, recalling a community-theater presentation in Redwood Falls: "My dear friend Mark was the Cowardly Lion in 'The Wizard of Oz.' The undisputed star of the show was a fantastic Wicked Witch. When she entered the auditorium, the lights would flicker, her cackles filled the air, and kids cowered beside Mom and Dad.

"At one point, the Cowardly Lion ran in fear of the witch off the stage into the audience. He crouched close to me and nervously played with his tail. The little girl next to me patted his arm reassuringly and said: 'Don't worry, Mr. Lion. It's only a play.' "

The Woman in Shell Lake: "Last night, my 4-year-old son and I watched *The Wizard of Oz.* When they got to the chase through the castle, my son looked at me and said: 'Mom, that witch is trying to get that girl, that dog, that scarecrow, that lion and that gas tank!' "

BULLETIN BOARD NOTES: He does keep saying: "Oiiiiillll caaaannnnn!" How's a 4-year-old to know that the Tin Man isn't simply introducing himself?

Mary of Highland Park: "My little 2½-year-old and I were outside after a big rain, and the wind blew, and it blew little raindrops down on my little boy's head. He stopped where he was, and he looked up and said: 'Mama, those trees are *spitting* on me.'"

Rod of White Bear Lake: "We have a large ash tree right outside our back door—a sliding-glass door. This fall, the tree lost almost all of its leaves overnight.

"The next morning, my 3-year-old daughter—who apparently didn't remember the previous fall—gasped in amazement at the sight of the barren tree. She called to her mom and pointed at the tree. Then a worried look came across her face. She paused for a moment and suddenly blurted: 'Tyler did that!'

"Tyler is her 6-year-old brother."

Jill of Lakeville: "My 10-year-old daughter's hamster died, and she was in her room crying, and I was in her room comforting her.

"Her 5-year-old brother, Tommy, walked in and said: 'What happened?'

"I said: 'JoLynda's hamster died, Tommy. What do you say to her?'—hoping for some expression of sympathy from him.

"Instead, he put his hands on his hips and yelled: 'I didn't *do* it!'"

Mary Conroy of Plymouth: "Our daughter Rosalie, who was 4, was sitting on her daddy's lap when she let out a large posterior breeze. We call them 'bombs' in our family.

"Her dad said: 'What do you *say*?'

"She quickly responded: 'Mom did it.'"

Ruth of Newport: "When my daughter was 2, we had a really horrible landlord at our apartment building. He would scream at the kids and threaten 'em, and one day he came into the parking lot and yelled at all of the little kids that were riding their Big Wheels in the parking area.

"He parked his car and came up to the building, and my 2-year-old little girl came up and said: 'Hi, there, you silly little man!'

"I think he would have blown up right there, like a bomb"—Ruth laughs a quietly mirthful laugh—"if he had been a bomb, anyway."

Wolfie of "beautiful Highland Park": "My 4-year-old daughter came home from preschool and said that a little boy came up to her and said: 'You're crabby! You're crabby!'

"And she replied: 'I'm not crabby. I just don't like you.'"

Mike of St. Paul: "My wife was in the kitchen doing dishes, and one of our kids, Melissa, who was about 3 or 4 at the time, was mad at Mary and came out and started hitting her on the leg. So Mary talks to her and says: 'Well, if you want to hit something, don't hit people; hit the cushions on the sofa.'

"So Mary goes back to doing dishes, and about a minute later, Melissa comes dragging the sofa cushion into the kitchen—and starts hitting Mary in the legs with the cushion."

Gene of Cottage Grove: "Our daughter and son-in-law just bought an old farmhouse over in Wisconsin and are in the process of fixing it up. This is a major undertaking: jack up the floors, plaster the walls and ceilings, new kitchen cabinets, new windows, new furnace, etc., etc.

"There were these wires sticking out of the living-room wall, and I made a sarcastic comment to my daughter: 'How nice that you've painted the wires to match the wall.' She said she didn't even know what the wires were for, and I said they must be for the furnace thermostat.

"About a half-minute later, my 3-year-old grandson, Jake, came out of the kitchen and said: 'Here it is, Poppa.' He was holding up his dad's Thermos bottle. He must have thought I asked: 'Where is the Thermos at?'

"God, I love that little guy."

Kelly of Stacy: "About a week ago, I discovered this really horrible smell coming from under my kitchen cupboard, and I couldn't find what it was.

"My two boys, Adam and Brendan, were investigating last night, and I heard them holler: 'We found it!' I heard Adam go: 'Well, I don't know. Ask Mama.'

"It was this Playmate cooler—you know, like a Thermos—and it had mold in it.

"And my son Brendan, who's 6, came to me and he goes: 'Mama, is mold alive?'

"And I said: 'Yeah. It is.'

"And he goes: 'When I take off the top and look at it, is it lookin' back at me?'

"Isn't that cute?"

Anne Fisher of White Bear Lake: "This past weekend, I was baby-sitting at my neighbors' house. I was walking over there, and the two little girls were out on the front porch.

"Amanda, who's 3, was looking out onto the grass, and their sprinklers had just turned off, so the porch light was reflecting off it, and the grass was glittery.

"She pointed out into the yard, and she goes: 'Look! There's diamonds in the grass!'

"I thought that was really sweet."

Anna M. Cracker of St. Paul: "When my daughter was a small child, she saw a jet plane go over, leaving a trail of white smoke.

"She said, 'Momma, it scratched the sky.'"

Tim of St. Paul: "I was going to Europe last year, and before I left, we had a party. My older sister said to me: 'Well, Tim, every time we see the moon, we'll think of you.'

"And my 3-year-old niece looked up at me with huge eyes, in astonishment, and said: 'You're going to the moon?'"

Svenska of White Bear Lake: "Years ago, my 2½-year-old son was sitting in his high chair, and he pointed out the window at a new moon.

"He said: 'Look at the fingernail in the sky, Mommy.'"

Lori of Elk River: "I just made some juice with my 3½-year-old son. We're trying a new kind of pulpless orange juice. He took one taste and said: 'Hey, this tastes good! And there's no hangnails in it!'"

Margaret of Menomonie, Wis.: "When my son was about 3 years old, he wandered into the bathroom one day when I was just getting out of the tub. This was right after the holiday season, when I had definitely indulged too much in the sweets, so I had a little pot on me there.

"My son walks in the door, and he was looking at me sort of curiously for a while, and then he said: 'Hey mom! How come your butt's in the front?'

"I never indulged that much again."

Cutie of St. Paul: "It was Grandma's Day, and as we were taking Grandma home after shopping and eating, my son Michael, who was then about 4, asked why he had a dimple on his cheek. As I was trying to figure out how to explain it to him so he'd understand, Grandma piped up and said that's where the angel had kissed him before he was born.

"The backseat of the car got very, very quiet, so I glanced in the rear-view mirror to see why—and Michael was just sittin' there with his mouth hangin' open. I knew that wasn't gonna be the end of this, but he was quiet for the time, so we just went on our way and dropped Grandma off, carried in all of her packages, and did all of the neat things that you do when you're at Grandma's house. And then we set off for home.

"We were no more than two houses away from Grandma's when Michael asked if he really got his dimple from an angel. Now, being a good mom and not wanting to lie, I said: 'Well, that's what Grandma said.'

"And as we waited at the stop sign, Michael looked me right in the eye and said: 'You mean an angel kissed Dad's butt?'

"Now, being a good mom and not wanting to lie, I said: 'You'd better ask Grandma that one.'"

Wolfie of "scenic Highland Park": "Recently we were having pancakes for breakfast on a Saturday morning, and the syrup was at the low end—just about out. And our 4-year-old heard the sound that the plastic bottle makes when you squeeze it and it's getting mostly air out, and she said: 'Boy, that sounds like a butt!'"

Sloe Gin of Eagan: "I've got a 4-year-old daughter who was opening up a two-liter pop a few days ago—and upon hearing the burp, she said: 'Mom, it pooped!'"

Grandma of Rosemount: "I baby-sit my two young grandsons; they're 3½ and 2½.

"Yesterday morning, we were outside looking at the beautiful fall colors, and over the house came a huge flock of geese; there was one way in the front, and about three or four V formations following.

"My 3½-year-old grandson pointed up and said: 'Look at that pile of geese, Grandma.'

"And I said: 'Yeah, I see. And listen to the noise they're making!'

"And my grandson says: 'Oh, you know what they're sayin', Grandma. They're sayin': "Wait for me! Wait for me!" ' "

L.A. of Cottage Grove: "The other day, I was driving down Warner Road along the Mississippi with my 4-year-old daughter, and she saw the big barges with the fiberglass covers that are all different colors.

"Now, I've always thought that these were incredibly ugly and garish, but I've got a completely new perspective.

"When my daughter pointed at them, she said: 'Look, Mom! Ice-cream boats!'

"There's something wonderful about thinking of huge barges full of ice cream floating down the Mississippi."

McGee of St. Paul: "My 5-year-old came home and said he had a prostitute teacher for the day. So, naturally, I had to correct him."

Trish of St. Paul: "My sister and brother-in-law were driving with their four kids, and my nephew who's in first grade was reading the juice box that he was drinking out of. He said: 'Hey, Mom! Look! This is made from 100 percent pure concrete.'

"And my other nephew, who's a little bit older, said: 'No, Matt. Concentrate!'

"And Matt said: 'I *am* concentrating!' "

Sue K. of New Richmond, Wis.: "A couple years ago, my sister was walking up the driveway with her little boy, Sam. I think he was 4 at the time. He was pointing to the big flower bushes along the driveway, and he says: 'Mama, what are these?'

"She says: 'Peonies.'

"He points to another one, and he says: 'Mama, what are these?'

"She says: 'Peonies.'

"They were visiting in the back yard for a little while with Grandma—and then she missed Sam, and she went looking for him, and there he had his zipper down and was going to the bathroom on the peony bushes. My sister said: 'Sammy, what are you doing?'

"And he said: 'You *said* to pee on these!'—so he did."

Jean of West St. Paul: "Many years ago, when my little boy was about 3½, my husband, as he often did, brought a lonesome college student home for supper. I served a chocolate sundae with peanuts on top, and my little boy said: 'What are those?'

"And I said: 'Peanuts.'

"And he laughed and said: 'I have peanuts in my pants and peanuts on my sundae!' "

The Cheese Lady of the East Side: "I was making gingerbread boys with my 2½-year-old son, and I let him put on the cinnamon candies. So he put an eye on, and another eye on, and then he put on the belly button.

"And then he put on the penis."

Alex's Mom of St. Paul: "Alex has progressed to big-boy underwear, and he was telling his grandmother all about them on the phone. Excitedly, he told them they were red, had the Tasmanian Devil on them, and had a pocket in the front.

"I'll explain later to him what the pocket is really for."

BULLETIN BOARD ADVISES: Better sooner than later.

Tracy of Highland Park: "On Thanksgiving Day, my family was here, and my fiance's family was here. We all sat around the dinner table saying what we were thankful for.

"We came to our 4-year-old nephew, and we said: 'Sam, what are you thankful for today?'

"He thought about it for a few seconds, and then he said: 'I'm thankful for ... my ... penis!'

"His parents denied having coached him to say that."

BULLETIN BOARD SAYS: We certainly hope they were telling the truth.

Berniece of West St. Paul: "Thanksgiving Day, I had my family over for dinner, and my grandson Michael's uncle asked him how old he was.

"Michael says: 'I'm 4.'

"And his uncle says: 'When are you going to be 5?'

"And Michael says: 'Well, when I'm done with 4.'"

M. of Inver Grove Heights: "When my son was 4 years old, I overheard him asking a middle-aged neighbor how old she was.

"Later, as I was explaining to him that it wasn't polite to have done this, he looked at me and said, rather indignantly: 'Well, she asked *me . . . first!*'"

Riley of Maplewood: "My little 4-year-old granddaughter Rebecca came over, and she was fascinated with my garden. We went back there, and I have a bumper crop of carrots.

"And I says: 'Look, Rebecca. There's carrots in here'—and I dug one out for her.

"She looks at me and says: 'Why did you put it in the dirt?'

"Aren't kids fun?"

Cheryl the Domestic Engineer of Newport: "My 10-year-old and I were cooking dinner together. I'd made a beautiful tossed salad—chopped the vegetables and put 'em in the bowl.

"I say to him: 'Toss the salad.'

"I proceeded to cook the dinner, and then he says: 'Mom, I tossed the salad.'

"He'd tossed it! It was in the garbage!"

Judy of the East Side: "A couple of years ago, my son was 4. I work a lot with polyester fiberfill; it comes in 15-ounce bags. It's real puffy stuff, and you can pull it apart and shred it until it looks like little pieces of snow.

"Anyway, one night, I accidentally left an open bag of it on my sewing chair and went into the kitchen to make supper. I came out and found that my son had found the open bag. There was snow all over the living room and the dining room.

"I looked at him and he said: 'Mom, it snowed in here.'

"So I said: 'Honey, I want you to pick every bit of this up and put it back in the bag.'

"He said: 'OK, Mom.'

"So I left the room, and he came in a few minutes later with a bag full of it and said: 'Now, what shall I do with it?'

"And I said: 'Go put it back where it was.'

"So I came out of the kitchen a couple of minutes later, and there it was—spread out all over the house, again."

Tallulah of Mac-Groveland: "I was driving home from work recently, a week or two ago, and I see my 9-year-old son, Kelse, and his buddy out raking leaves in the front yard. And I'm thinking: 'Now, isn't that great? That's what Minnesota falls are all about: kids outside raking up leaves and jumping into the piles.'

"So I pull around to the garage, go up to the house, start making supper. And maybe a half-hour later, Kelse comes running into the house, all excited, saying: 'Mom! Mom! You gotta come out! You gotta see this fantastic leaf pile we have! It's absolutely awesome!'

"So I think: 'Oh, OK. I'll go out and take a look.' I mean, how much more could he have raked up in 20 or 30 minutes? Anyway, I go out—and there is this truly awesome, *humungo* leaf pile stretching across practically our entire front yard. I couldn't *believe* all of the leaves in our front yard.

"So I said: 'Kelse, my God! How did you get all those leaves in just the last half-hour?'

"And he goes: 'Well, Mom, remember Andy was doing the neighbors' yard?' Andy's his older brother. 'Well, we brought all those bags over and dumped those all out. And remember Dad had done some of the leaves—those five or six bags in back? Well, we dumped all those out, too. Isn't this *great?*'

"He proceeded to thoroughly enjoy jumping in them—he and his friend.

"I must admit: I wasn't too upset. I thought: That's what being a kid in a Minnesota fall is all about."

Dawn of Stillwater, on a snow day: "My 10-year-old, Jon, was very appreciative of the powers-that-be who closed Stillwater's schools due to the weather.

" 'Mom, who is in charge of closing the schools?' he asked the second morning—still snuggling under his covers.

"Well, I explained, the superintendent of your school, David Wettergren, had made that decision.

" 'Mom,' he said, in all earnest, 'he's a good man.' "

The Great Gonzo of Oakdale: "My 7-year-old daughter had to draw a picture of something that she enjoys doing. She came in the house and brought me this wonderful picture of one child sliding down a hill on a sled, with wonderful trees and snow and everything. And the caption read: 'My brother and I sledding.'

"When I asked my daughter where her brother was, since there was only one person on the sled, she responded: 'Oh, he got cold and went inside.' "

Karyn of St. Paul Park: "Last winter, when I was driving my son to day care on a snowy morning when all the trees were covered with snow, I pointed out the window and said: 'Look how pretty they look!'

"And he said: 'Yeah, Mom. They look like doughnuts!' I thought about it a moment—and yeah, I guess they did look like powdered-sugar doughnuts.

"And then he said: 'But when they don't have snow, they *don't* look like doughnuts.' "

Grandmother Jess of Maplewood: "One day, my son's family was on the way home from church, and they went by a doughnut shop. My daughter-in-law said: 'Should we get some doughnuts?'

"And my little grandson—5 at that time—said: 'Doughnuts make your brown eyes blue.' "

Jim of St. Paul: "My wife and I were sittin' at the kitchen table one day when my sister-in-law and nephew came in.

"Little Dan said to me: 'Your eyes are blue. My ma's eyes are blue. And my eyes are blue.'

"He looked at my wife, whose eyes are brown, and said: 'What color is the sky to *you?*' "

Morning Glory of Eau Claire, Wis.: "My little daughter Sally is turning 5 at the end of March.

"She came into this world with amazing, beautiful eyes. When she was 3, the clerk at the health-food store asked her: 'Where'd you get those big blue eyes?'

"Sal put her hands on her hips, and she replied: 'I've had them for a long time.'"

Mike of Lake Elmo: "My son Mike Jr.—born a redhead to two brunette parents—was the butt of the old 'Where'd you get the red hair, sonny?' question at just about every gathering—wedding, funeral and such—that we went to.

"At one family gathering, when he was about 8 years old, an out-of-town uncle tousled his hair and roared for everyone to hear: 'Where'd you get the red hair, sonny?'

"He did me proud when he pulled away and proudly announced: 'It came with the head.'"

Janet of Apple Valley: "My daughter, who is 4 years old, has a few hand puppets, and she loves to play pretend games. Yesterday, she took two hand puppets and asked me to play with her. She was the father, a crocodile, and I was the daughter, a little bear. We made conversations.

"In a little girl's voice, I asked her: 'Daddy, where's my mommy?'

"She answered: 'She died.' And I pretended to rub my little bear eyes and cried: 'Boo-hoo-hoo.' She comforted me by saying: 'Don't cry, baby. I'll bring you to heaven to see her someday.'

"Trying to give her a hard time, I then asked her: 'Daddy, how come I'm your baby—and you look like a crocodile and I look like a bear?'

"Without missing a beat, she replied: 'You look like your mother.'"

Gretchen of Lake Elmo: "My 6-year-old daughter—about a year and a half ago—was sitting around with me and my mom right after we had eaten lunch. Some people had been talking about how much my daughter looked like me. I don't think she does, but I thought maybe she looked like my mother.

"I said to my mom: 'Do you think she looks like you?'

"And my mom said: 'Well, I don't know. I don't have noodles all over my face.'

"And my daughter said to my mother: 'Yeah, and I don't have wrinkles all over *my* face.'"

Dori of Inver Grove Heights: "I had my 4-year-old nephew, Conor, and 9-year-old niece, Bridget, over. We were sitting at the table, and I was saying to them that Conor looks so much like his older brother, Timmy. Then I said: 'But I don't know whose ears he has.'

"And Conor said: 'I have my own ears!'"

Grammy Kay of St. Paul: "I'm calling about my 3-year-old grandson, who five days ago got a brand-new baby sister. He went to the hospital to see his new baby sister, Alyssa.

"Mom was saying: 'Gee, she doesn't look like me.'

"Dad said: 'I don't think she looks like me, either.'

"After studying the baby's face a while, Chris said: 'I think she looks like the neighbor.'

"Mom laughed so hard she almost ripped her stitches out."

Dorothy of Forest Lake: "When my son was about 2 years old, we visited my aunt and uncle on a farm up by Bruno. That evening, we were out in the barn watching my aunt and uncle milking cows—the old-fashioned way. That, in itself, nearly popped my son's eyeballs.

"Suddenly, a cow lifted her tail and done what cows do in the gutter. My son watched in total amazement, then asked my aunt: 'How do cows wipe?'

"My aunt nearly fell off her three-legged milkstool."

Short Change of Stillwater: "My son, who is 2 years old, was getting out of the bathtub the other day, and he took his two thumbs and pointed at his chest and said: 'Look, Mommy! I have small nickels.'

"And then he looked at me and said: 'Mommy, you have big nickels.'

"But what really made me laugh is:

"He said: 'Daddy has bigger nickels than both of us.'"

Kathy of Somerset, Wis.: "I was commenting to my 8-year-old son the other night that he was very much like his dad.

"He said: 'Yeah. I'm a chip off the old chunk.'"

Mary B. of Blue Earth: "Our 3-year-old son, Mark, sat in a grocery cart as I pushed him down an aisle. We came upon a young man stocking shelves who was wearing a long ponytail and an earring in one ear.

"Upon hearing this young man's deep voice speaking to another employee, Mark exclaimed: 'Look, Mommy! There's a boy with a girl on top!'"

Amy of St. Paul: "About 10 years ago, when my niece Becca was 3 or 4, I showed her a picture of her dad taken before she was born. In the picture, he had very long hair and no beard. Since Becca's birth, he has had short hair and a beard—so I didn't think she would recognize him.

"I asked her if she knew who was in the picture, and she said: 'Yes, that's my daddy when he was a lady.'"

Tom of St. Louis Park: "My wife needed a hand in the kitchen, so she asked my older daughter, Sarah Lorraine, to run upstairs and get me. Sarah returned, saying: 'Daddy's busy.'

"'Daddy's busy? Doing what?' my wife asked.

"'He's busy sleeping,' said Sarah, as she left the room."

Grandma Ruth of White Bear Lake: "My 3-year-old granddaughter Katie stays with us on school days. The other day, her 15-year-old sister, Becky, had the day off school; took care of Katie, and also did a great job cleaning house.

"I asked Katie the next day: 'Did you help Becky clean the house?'

"She answered: 'Yes. I took a nap.'"

Michele of Inver Grove Heights: "My daughter was about 3 years old, maybe 4 years old at the time, and I'd just given her a bath. She wanted an orange, so I gave her an orange, and, of course, she got all sticky from the juice. She started wiping her shirt with her hands.

"I looked at her and yelled: 'Brooke, use your head!'

"She started wiping her hands all over her hair."

Michele A. of Chokio: "I have a little girl named Molly, and the other day, I was trying to put a ponytail in Molly's hair. She would not hold still, so I put a hand on either side of her head, positioned it just the way I wanted it and said: 'There! Hold your head just like that.'

"So she put her hands up to her head and held her head."

Mormor of Maplewood: "Our 3-year-old granddaughter, Lauren, was visiting us on Father's Day and was downstairs proudly saying the alphabet for her grandfather.

"She finished, very proud of herself, and Grandpa said: 'All right, Lauren. Now say it backwards.'

"She paused a minute, looked him in the eye, turned around—and, with her back towards him, proceeded to recite the alphabet."

D.M.J. of St. Paul: "Recently, my husband bought me a treadmill to work out on. My 3-year-old grandson, Mikey, was over, and I went down in the back room to walk on my treadmill. He'd never seen me walk on it before; he hadn't seen it.

"He comes running into the room, and he goes: 'Grandma! What you doing?'

"I said: 'I'm walking on my treadmill, Mike. I'm getting some exercise.'

"Looked at me for a minute, and he goes: 'Well, where you going?'

"I started to laugh, and I said: 'I'm not going anywhere. I'm staying right here.'

"Kinda looked at me again and said: 'You goin' to the park?'

"I said: 'Yeah, Mike. Grandma's going to the park.'

"He had brought some toys with him into the room, so he started playing with those—and a little while later, I turned around to walk backwards on my treadmill, to get some exercise a little differently. He looked up at me, and he goes: 'Grandma, you goin' home now?'

"I started to laugh and said: 'Yeah, Mike. Grandma's going home.' "

The Original Newcomer of St. Paul: "I was visiting a prospective school for my daughter and heard the following story from the kindergarten teacher:

"She was helping one of her students choose the child's best schoolwork for a portfolio to give to the first-grade teacher. After the kindergarten teacher encouraged the child to 'put her best foot forward,' the little girl asked: 'What should I do with my other foot?' "

Julie of Osceola, Wis.: "My little sister, Amy, was baby-sitting for good friends of our family; they were having a birthday party for their 4-year-old little girl, Mallory. It was a swimming party, so the mom wanted my little sister to come over and help out and watch the little kids.

"They were out playing with Amy, and one girl said to her: 'Amy, look! I can hop on one foot!'

"And another little girl, the queen of upmanship, says: 'Oh, yeah? Well, I can hop on two!' "

Allison's Mommy: "I took Allison to the doctor for her 2-year-old check. They do coordination tests, like stacking blocks, and they watch and see if they walk properly.

"And then the doctor said: 'Allison, can you stand on one foot for me?'

"And she walked over and stood on his foot."

June of Blaine's Brother of Hugo: "I never thought I'd be callin' in a cute kid story, but here goes:

"My sister and her family just got back from Florida. They were swimmin' in a pool at the hotel, and my sister was watching her 5-year-old, Matt, makin' his way along the edge to the deep end.

"She warned him that he can't touch his feet at the 8-foot deep end—and with a determined look, he reaches down and touches his feet and says: 'Mom, look! I can *too* touch my feet at the deep end.'

"Never underestimate a kid."

Missy the Bartender of Mahtomedi: "I stay home with my two daughters during the day; I have a 5-year-old and a 3-year-old.

"Little girls tend to be very whiny, and we were having one of these days when they were whining and whining and whining. I wanted to get away from them for a minute, so I went into the bath-room and shut the door—and my 3-year-old opened the door just a little bit, and she got real whiny and said: 'Mommy?'

"I looked at her and I said: 'You want Mommy to go to an insane asylum? Is that what you want? Mommy's gonna go to an insane asylum, Casey.'

"And she looked up at me and got this whiny look on her face and said: 'I come wiiiiith!'

"I just looked at her and said: 'Rest my case, kiddo.'"

Mary Kay of Arden Hills: "Sometimes when I'm alone with my 3½-year-old daughter, Katie, I feel that I'm in the presence of someone far more wise and noble than myself.

"Today she reminded me to keep my small annoyances in perspective.

"This morning, when we went downstairs to the playroom, a familiar mixture of despair, anger and exhaustion engulfed me. This room, which had looked so inviting just yesterday, looked as if a bomb had gone off. Every Lego, every puzzle piece, every accessible toy had been trashed.

"Katie must have understood my mounting frustration, because before I could gather enough steam to scream, she gently slipped her hand into mine, looked up to me and said: 'That's OK, Mommy. Me will clean it up nice. I love you, Mommy.'

"She skillfully melted my fury."

The Lug Nut of Woodbury: "Yesterday, I was having a very crabby day—and my 4-year-old said: 'If it was summer, I'd pick you a flower, Mom.' And that sure made me feel a lot better."

Grandpa Fabian of West St. Paul: "One day, while our 4-year-old granddaughter, Jessica, was over visiting, she started to get pretty unruly. She had been driving over her grandmother's flower bed with her trike. She was warned several times to stop.

"Finally, Grandma took Jessica's chin in her hand, looked into her eyes and said: 'If you do that one more time, young lady, you'll be going to bed to take a nap.'

"Jessica replied: 'That's OK, Grandma. I'm a little tired anyways.'"

El of St. Paul: "My niece from Louisiana was visiting me for two weeks and had a box of goodies—crackers, cookies and so forth— for the kids to eat on the trip.

"She put the box in my rec room downstairs, and one day she went down to get a box of crackers and discovered it was empty—as was the cookie box.

"She asked Levi, the 3-year-old, what happened. He said: 'I ate them.'

"So she said: 'You sit on the bottom step and decide how I should punish you. You know you didn't ask for them, and you have to be punished. So you decide.'

"He sat there a minute or two, and he says: 'Well, I guess you'd better spank me.'

"She says: 'As soon as I finish folding these clothes, I'll spank you.'

"He waited about a minute, and he said: 'I've got a better idea. I'm pretty tired tonight, so I think we'd better wait 'til morning.'"

Pinky of Woodbury: "Today is my only baby child's birthday. He's 27 years old, so he's been gone from home a long time—but I've been thinking about him today.

"When my son was about 3½ years old, he was very upset with me for one reason or another, and he decided that he was going to run away from home. So he packed up a little bag and got the stuff that he wanted in it and proceeded to announce that he was leaving.

"He said: 'I'm leaving. Goodbye'—and he just slammed out the front door.

"Fifteen seconds later, he came back in and said: 'I want the checkbook.'"

H.B. of Oakdale: "I want to tell you a little story about my daughter, when she was 5 years old.

"She got very angry with me one day and said she was gonna run away from home.

"We went through supper, and she was still sittin' there pouting, and I says: 'You still running away?'

"She says: 'Yes.' So she got her suitcase and packed it. I asked if she needed any help, and she says: 'No.'

"So she dragged her suitcase out of her room and went outside. I held the door open for her. And she hesitated, and I said: 'What's the matter, honey?'

"She said: 'It's gonna get dark pretty soon, so I'll wait for tomorrow.'

"That was the end of her running away."

Grandma Bette of Shoreview: "Mom and Dad talking with Julie, age 8.

"Mom says: 'Just think, Julie. In 10 years, you'll be old enough to leave home.'

"Julie replies: 'Why would I want to leave home, when my blanket is here?'

"Makes good sense when you think about it."

Lisa of St. Paul: "When my son, who is now 10, was about 3 years old, I picked him up from day care and, like I always did at the end of the day, asked him how his day went. He said that they'd talked about what they would be when they grew up.

"After he sat there for a while, just sort of looking out the window in the car, he looked at me and said: 'Mom, you know what I want to be when I grow up?'

"I said: 'No, what?'

"He said: 'I want to be a stranger.'"

BULLETIN BOARD REPLIES: Funny thing. That's pretty much how it usually works out, isn't it?

Andrea of Maplewood: "My 2-year-old nephew, Josh, has done many adorable things, but this one always seems to stick in my head. (Happens to be 1 in the morning, and I happen to be thinking about it.)

"One day, he took my hand and led me into his room. He took out several little plastic animals to play with. Without looking at it, I grabbed one, and, pretending to be the animal, I said: 'Hi! My name is . . . '—and then I stopped. I realized I didn't even know what the animal was.

"I stared at Josh, and I stared at the animal, and I smiled foolishly, not knowing what it was. He waited for an answer and finally, giving me a consoling smile, he whispered in my ear: 'My name is elk.'

"I said: 'Yes. Why, of course it is!'

"I mean, I knew the kid was real smart, but I didn't know he had passed me up already."

Baby Jupiter's Sister, Beanie Burger of Westby, Wis.: "A few days ago, my 6-year-old daughter, Erica, and I were waiting for her school bus to come and pick her up at our dairy farm.

"My daughter is a business-minded person who looks at everything she does as another step forward in her career as a child, so we have some interesting conversations while waiting for the bus.

"On this day, I was asking her about some friends of hers—one being a boy who tends to be sort of a rascal at times. She said that he had been naughty the day before and had had to put a dollar on Mrs. M——'s desk. I thought it was unusual that the teacher had taken up a cash-forfeiture policy for wrongdoings, but Erica assured me that it was fake money.

"Mrs. M—— was teaching money values and gave each child five fake $1 bills. For each assigned duty, the child was then paid more of these fake dollars—but for slacking off duties or goofing off, Mrs. M—— was to be paid a fake dollar.

"I asked Erica how many dollars she had. Nine was her answer. She went on to say that she had never had to pay Mrs. M—— and was the only kid in the class who never had to pay.

"I praised her for that, saying how proud I was of her good behavior.

"She said: 'Mrs. M—— said the same thing. But I told her: "I'm a dairy farmer. I can't afford to be giving my money away!" ' "

Todd of Stillwater: "My 8-year-old and my 5-year-old were called into the principal's office for getting involved in a name-calling battle on the school bus.

"As we were dealing with this issue before bed, I asked my kids what names they had called the other children.

"My 5-year-old came up with a relatively standard name used by grade-school kids.

"My 8-year-old told me that she had used a name that the other kids wouldn't understand: 'I called them *lithos kopro*.'

"I asked her what that was, and she said it was Greek for fossilized dung."

BULLETIN BOARD NOTES: Hence the English word coprolite—*meaning fossilized excrement.*

Hey, you learn something new—or, in this case, very, very old—every day.

JB's Wife: "Yesterday we received a note in the mail telling us that our second-grader (now nicknamed 'Fudgy') was in a fight at school. So last night I had a talk with him to get the whole story.

"He went into a detailed report telling me that it happened last Friday morning when they were coming into the school and that they got picked up in the hall and sent to the principal's office. He then explained exactly what he did, what the other kid did, what he did, what the other kid did, etc.

"When he was all done, I wanted to find out if he understood the mistakes he had made, so I asked him: 'Do you know where you went wrong here?'

"Fudgy got a funny look on his face, and without hesitation he replied: 'Yeah. It was in the hall near the nurse's office, right by the pencil machine.'"

Roxanne of St. Paul: "My 6-year-old son, John, goes to Kindercare in downtown St. Paul. They went over to Rice Park and played tee-ball.

"I said to him: 'How'd you hit the ball?'

"He looked at me and says: 'With a bat, Mom.'

"Don't you think that's cute?"

Gordon of Inver Grove Heights: "The other day, one of our little neighborhood kids happened upon our doorstep and told me that he played baseball that day. Actually, it was tee-ball.

"I asked him: 'What position do you play?'

"And he said: 'Well, mostly sitting.'"

Granny Annie of Macalester-Groveland: "My almost-2-year-old grandson spent almost six hours at the fair last Friday—the greater part of his time sitting in his stroller. On Saturday, when he came to visit, I asked him: 'Eli, what did you see at the fair yesterday?'

"His answer: 'Legs.'

"There's an honest answer for you.

"These kids have given me the greatest laughs I've ever had."

Grammy of St. Paul: "I was talking to my daughter, telling her I needed to find some purple yarn.

"Later that day, my grandson, who's 4 years old, called out: 'Grammy, did you find your purple yarn?'

"I said: 'Yes! I found it at Wal-Mart!'

"And he replied: 'Is that where you lost it?'"

Anne of West St. Paul: "My daughter was going to buy her little 4-year-old a two-piece bathing suit, but she didn't have quite enough money, so she was going to put it on Will Call. When she went to the Will Call desk, she said: 'I'll pay for half of it now.'

"On their way home, my little granddaughter said to her mother: 'Which half am I going to get?'"

M.A. of St. Paul: "I have a friend named Shelly with a 4-year-old son, and she was explaining the Irish and St. Patrick's Day to him. *[BULLETIN BOARD NOTES: All in one session? The poor child.]* She told him that he was half Irish, and of course he wanted to know: 'Which half?'"

BULLETIN BOARD REPLIES (in the spirit o' the o'casion): Why, lad, the better half, o' course!

Marie of Hugo: "On the Feast of St. Nicholas, my three kids each put one of their shoes outside their bedroom door, in the hope that St. Nick would visit and leave them a treat. The next morning, when I was driving my 7-year-old son—also named Nicholas—to school, I said: 'Well, Nick, I see that St. Nicholas came last night.'

"He said: 'Yeah! Finally a saint named after me.'

"You gotta love 'em."

Just A Mom of St. Paul: "Today being St. Nicholas Eve, my kids all put their shoes out. My daughter pulled out the nastiest, ickiest sandal from this past summer; it's just awful-looking.

"I asked her how come she pulled out such an icky-looking shoe, and she said: 'Well, just in case he gives me coal, I don't want to ruin my *good* shoe.'"

Linda of Hastings: "Reading Just A Mom's story made me think of when my oldest son was in kindergarten and came home from school with the story of St. Nicholas Eve. That tradition was not something my family celebrated, so it was new to me. He told me that if you put your shoes out at night, St. Nicholas would fill them.

"I said: 'OK. We can do that.'

"So that evening, gettin' ready to tuck him into bed, all the way up and down the hall was every shoe and every boot in the house. Had to be 20, 25 boots."

Tim of Maple Grove: "My wife was arguing the other day with my son Joe, who is 6, about getting Joe to put his boots on.

"Mom said that Joe should get his boots on because moms knew everything.

"Joe argued back and forth about putting his boots on, and finally he said: 'If you know, everything, Mom, what killed the dinosaurs?'"

Cheri of Woodbury: "My daughter and I and her father were down visiting her grandparents in Waseca. My daughter is hip to all the dinosaurs and their names, and can just rattle 'em off one after another.

"Her grandmother had never heard her pronounce the dinosaurs' names, so she proceeded to ask her. My daughter rattled off stegosaurus, tyrannosaurus rex, brontosaurus, pterodactyl—and her grandmother was very, very impressed.

"She said: 'Well, Katie Jane, where were all the people when the dinosaurs were around?'

"Katie shrugged her shoulders—she's 3 years old—and put her hands up in the air and said: 'I don't know. In a meeting.'"

Summer of Shoreview: "Some friends from out of town just visited with their preschool daughter. They'd had a birthday party for her, and the parents thought it would be kind of fun to have a pinata. So they went to the store and looked at the pinatas; they chose the Barney pinata 'cause the kids are all so wild about him.

"Well, big mistake. The kids came to the party, and none of them wanted to hit the pinata. I guess it was sort of like having a Virgin Mary pinata at a church picnic.

"One girl finally did hit the pinata open, and the kids got their treats—but even she, after it was all over, asked if she could take the pieces home so she could fix Barney up."

Gram Millie of Anoka: "When my 4-year-old granddaughter was over to visit one day, she showed me her brand-new Barney shoes. They had Velcro closures, and she said to me: 'Grandma, do you know how these work?'

"And I said: 'Yes, I have a pair.'

"She said: 'Of Barney shoes?'"

Lucky Mama of St. Paul: "The other day, we were in the van, and my 20-month-old daughter was in the back seat, and my husband and I were holding hands, and she said: 'Don't hold hands with him! He's my husband!'

"I said: 'He's not your husband; he's your papa.'

" 'He's my husband! No hold hands!'

"I said: 'Papa is your papa! He's not your husband.'

"She was quiet for a minute, and then she said in this little voice: '*Barney's* my husband.' "

John & Jennifer of Lino Lakes: "Last night, we had put our 3½-year-old to bed. About 15 minutes later, she crept downstairs—explaining how she was not tired and couldn't sleep. We told her to go back up—and that she could get some of her favorite books and read in bed.

"She said: 'I can't read. I'm a child.' "

David B. of Hastings: "This morning at 3 o'clock, my daughter Joscelyn, who is 4 years old, came into our bedroom to tell us that she went potty but did not flush the toilet because she didn't want to wake us up."

Fran of Minneapolis: "We just had our not-quite-2-year-old little granddaughter overnight, and for some reason, she decided she did not want to sleep in her porta-crib; she wanted to sleep with Grandma.

"That was fine, but sometime during the night, she decided she was gonna pull open my eyelid and say: 'Hi, Grandma!'

"Once wasn't so bad, but three or four times? Next time, *I* sleep in the porta-crib."

Jim Fitzsimons of St. Paul: "I have a nephew who's 7 years old, and he was sleeping over with my parents. He got up—after being in bed for about an hour or so—and came out into the living room and said to Grammy and Papa: 'I can't sleep!'

"Both Grammy and Papa tried to convince him: 'Oh, you just go back into bed and give it a try. You'll fall asleep.'

"And my nephew said: 'I can't sleep in that bed!'

"And they asked him why not, and he said: 'I throwed up in it!' "

Lisa of Rochester: "One night, my daughter Jessica, who was 3 at the time, had a nightmare in the middle of the night and crawled into bed with us to sleep.

"In the morning, she said: 'Mommy, I think Daddy's a monster.'

"Surprised, I asked: 'Why is that?'

"To which my daughter replied: 'Because he growled all night.' "

Shannon of Inver Grove Heights: "I gave my 2½-year-old son a lemon bar for a treat, which he decided he didn't like, so he spit it into his hand and wanted to hand it to me.

"I said: 'Put it in the basket.'

"Son: 'No.'

"Mom: 'Then put it in the sink.'

"Son: 'No' (as he dumps it into my hand).

"Mom (with my hand out): 'Do I look like a basket or a sink?'

"Son (thinking about it very carefully): 'A sink!' "

Ann of Mendota Heights: "I was changing my 2½-year-old's diaper, and she said: 'Mom, or Mommy?'

"I asked: 'What did you say?'

"And she said: 'Mom, or Mommy?'

"And I said: 'What would you *like* to call me?'

"And she said: 'I think . . . the boss.' "

J.D. of Andover: "My sister, Barb, was traveling in her car with her daughter, Kilee-Ann, when she ended up behind an erratically driven car. The person kept slowing down and speeding up.

"Eventually, the car turned off the road, and Barb made the statement: 'That idiot!'

"Kilee-Ann then inquired: 'Where's the idiot?'

"Barb said: 'Oh, he turned off back there.'

"Whereupon Kilee-Ann told Barb: 'Dad knows him, too!' "

Diane of Blaine: "I took my 3½-year-old son to his preschool screening, and one of the teachers asked him what his mom does when she gets in the car. His reply was: 'She honks the horn at the jerks.' "

Margaret of Woodbury: "When my son was young, he was to write a composition—25 words or less—about his mother.

"He wrote: 'My mother cooks and yells.'"

BULLETIN BOARD NOTES: The lad was well on his way to becoming a fine writer.

We quote Principle of Composition No. 17 from the writer's bible, William Strunk Jr.'s and E.B. White's The Elements of Style: *"Omit needless words."*

Bonnie of Stillwater: "My 7-year-old son, Tommy, had a school assignment in which he was supposed to draw a picture of all of the members of his family doing something they enjoy. So he draws his dad playing broomball, his brother playing baseball. He draws himself walking the dog—and he draws me . . . sleeping in.

"I'm so embarrassed."

JB's Wife: "The other day, I found a note tucked away in my dresser. It was written by my youngest son a few years ago, when he was in first grade and just learning to read and write. Here's exactly what he wrote:

" 'My Mom is the best mom in the yunavrss. So good that sumtimss she plas with me. But if she dusint wont to I dot ckarr. I stl love hrr.

" 'Frum Ben'

"I'm so glad I saved this little note. It warms my heart every time I read it and reminds me what a blessing it is to have kids."

Carol of Oakdale: "I was just going through some papers that belong to my daughter—report cards, and things like that. She's now 22. And I came across this letter that she had to write for school when she was about second grade, and I had just gone back to work. I think it's priceless.

"It's entitled 'My Mom': 'My mom is a nice person. She has red hair and green eyes. Her hobby is shopping. She works a lot of the time. She doesn't like to cook so we usually have McDonald's. But my mom is my mom.'

"The teacher gave her an Excellent on it, and it just cracked me up—and it still does. I love it, and I wouldn't part with it."

Grandma Shirley of Cottage Grove: "This was on Thanksgiving:

"After we say grace, as we stand around our table laden with turkey and pumpkin pie and sweet potatoes and all kinds of goodies, we all give a reason that we are thankful. We start with the oldest and go on down to the youngest.

"When we got to the 3-year-old, the final one, he said: 'Thank God for McDonald's!'

"So much for turkey and pumpkin pie."

A Doting Grandma of Maplewood: "Our daughter was reading a children's book to her 3-year-old son, and along the way, he asked her to turn back a few pages so he could look at the picture of the cookie.

"Well, she couldn't remember any picture of a cookie, but she flipped back—and he said: 'There it is!'

"And she said: 'Honey, that's not a cookie. Think again. What can that be?'

"He looked at it, and he said: 'A marshmallow?'

"And she said: 'No. Think about a chicken. What does a chicken lay?'

"And he grinned happily and said: 'Nuggets!' "

Dr. I. of Eau Claire, Wis.: "When my son Douglas was about 4, his favorite food was chicken nuggets from McDonald's. One day, he asked: 'Daddy, were chicken nuggets once alive?'

"I responded: 'Yes, they were once chickens.'

"He looked puzzled.

" 'Very *little* chickens?' "

Lori of Forest Lake: "My niece has the chicken pox right now, and we were at Grandma's house together—trying to get my 3-year-old son exposed, just to get it over with.

"My mom was putting the medicine on her back—on the chicken pox all over—and a few hours later, my son comes walking up to his Nana, lifts his shirt in the back and says: 'Nana, will you feed my chickens, too?' "

Grandma Sue of Cottage Grove: "We were at Disneyland with our granddaughter Maggie, who is 6. She's a very friendly child and was standing in line talking with another adorable little girl—a little freckle-faced girl.

"Maggie got this worried look on her face, and she looked up and said: 'Grandma, can I get chicken pox twice?'"

Laurie of Dellwood: "I was baby-sitting for my little cousin Lindsay, when she was about 4 years old. We were having a nice little conversation about chicken pox, because my brother had it at the time. I asked her if she had ever had chicken pox. She looked really serious at me for a minute, and then she said: 'No, but I've had Chicken McNuggets before!'"

Kathy of Mendota Heights: "When I was in the Eagan McDonald's a few months ago with my three preschoolers, my oldest one, who's 4, accidentally threw away his Happy Meal toy.

"He started to cry a little bit, and I told him I wasn't going to dig through the trash; it was time to go. And he was still crying and whimpering and having a little bit of a temper tantrum as we were walking to the car.

"We were all the way across the parking lot when another little boy—who was only about 5 or 6—came running out after us and said: 'Here! Here! He can have *mine!*'

"I was just so overwhelmed with his kindness."

Lynn of St. Paul: "My 8-year-old just went away to camp for the first time. I was really worried that she'd miss me really bad, and I was telling her that she could write me a letter and that might help her feel better.

"We sent along some envelopes that were already addressed, and here's a letter I got back from her: 'Roses are red, violets are blue, what makes you think that I would miss you?'

"Cute, huh?"

The Original Newcomer of St. Paul: "My 5-year-old and I have a game where I'll tell her which way is one direction—for example, north—and she figures out which direction we're going.

"Recently we were playing this game during the sunset, and I told her that the sun sets in the west. When I asked her where the sun rises, she gave me a patronizing 'Aw, Mom' look and pointed straight up in the air."

The Home Creator of St. Paul: "My son Jack was out with a ball, bouncing it in the front yard, and I told him that if he lost the ball, he should come tell me—not go after it in the street, or anywhere else.

"A couple minutes later, he comes in; he says he can't find the ball. So I ask my daughter Leah to go out and see if she can help him find it.

"She comes in a minute later, laughing hysterically, and I said: 'What happened?'

"She said: 'Well, I asked him which way he threw it—so I could get an idea which direction to look in—and he pointed *up.*'"

LaVonne of Coon Rapids: "I have a cute kid story for you that illustrates the uselessness of scientific accuracy when it comes to the big questions:

" 'Mom, how did they make the world?' asked my 5-year-old son, Robby.

"Several choices came to mind:

"(A) The biblical version.

"(B) The Big Bang theory.

"(C) A flight of my own imagination involving, oh, let's say a giant out in space.

"I chose (B).

" 'Well,' I said, winding up, 'some people think there was a big explosion out in space a long time ago and that it sent a lot of big rocks spinning out all over the place. And they think that Earth and the moon and the sun and all the stars came from the explosion. They call it the Big Bang.'

"I was proud of my lucid, if simple-minded, explanation of serious scientific theory. Robby nodded sagely and thought a moment.

" 'After that explode,' he said, 'do you know how they made rain?'

"My mind raced to explain evaporation, but Robby beat me to it.

" 'A big giant out in space takes a watering can and pours water on a big flower, and the Earth is inside the flower, right?'

" 'Right,' I said.

"I like his answer a lot better than mine."

Grandma's of Lexington: "I've taken care of my grandson since he was 6 months old. I would say something like 'Grandma's going to give you a bath' or 'Grandma's got to go to the store'—and he has always called me 'Grandma's.' He's 6 years old now, and he still calls me Grandma's—and I love to hear that.

"He came home from kindergarten today and showed me some little pictures he had cut and glued, about the transformation of a caterpillar into a butterfly.

"I asked him to explain it to me, and he said: 'First, the caterpillar eats. Then he gets a stomachache. Then he gets real fat. Then he builds a coconut house. Then he sleeps—and when he wakes up, he turns into a butterfly. That's what caterpillars are supposed to do.'

"I love being his Grandma's, and I told him that last night. I'll never forget the smile I got."

Thidwick: "My 10-year-old daughter likes to make up stories. When she was flying back to the Twin Cities, she was looking out at the clouds and made up a story, which she told me about:

"There was a Cloud Boy, and the Cloud Boy was very lonely because he had no one to play with him—and he realized that he wouldn't be able to come down to Earth, because if he did come down to Earth, he would dissolve. Eventually, he became very happy because a little bird was flying up in the air and decided to become his friend.

"My suggestion was that maybe she could have an airplane, which would be friends to both the Cloud Boy and the little bird. She looked at me and said: 'Well, *Dad!* I wanted it to be *realistic!*' "

Anonymous of the Boonies: "Once upon a time, my small son was coloring in a coloring book—a purple rabbit.

"I asked: 'Did you ever see a purple bunny rabbit?'

"And he pops right back: 'I'm not coloring for real. I'm coloring for pretty!'

"Amen."

Brad of St. Louis Park: "My niece sent my mother-in-law a valentine on Valentine's Day, and it said: 'Dear Grandma, I love you like the flowers love the rain, like the bunny loves his carrot, and like a whale loves his snort hole. Love, Emily.' "

Kim of New Brighton: "My daughter Nicole has recently started buying her dad and I cards for all of the holidays. On Valentine's

Day, we received a card that, on the outside of the envelope, it read: 'This card contains so much love I had to sit on it to seal it.'

"She'll never know how much she's cherished."

BULLETIN BOARD REPLIES: Maybe so. But give it your best shot, OK?

Roberta of St. Paul: "My 4-year-old keeps making the most delightful mistake. She keeps telling me that she's going to get me something for St. Mother's Day.

"I just love it."

Normally Not Sentimental Mom of the West Side: "My 5-year-old daughter, who is at the pre-reading stage, likes to narrate the picture books from the illustrations. Last night, she was doing well reading an ABC book to me until she got stuck on 'V is for Valentine.'

"I gave her some clues: 'What holiday do you give cards that say "I love you" that start with the sound vuh-vuh-vuh?'

"She brightened. 'Vother's Day!' "

Loretta of Oakdale: "I have a little girl who's 3 years old. She was at my mom's house working on an alphabet puzzle—where you lift up the letters, and underneath is something that starts with that letter. Lift up A, and there's an apple: A is for apple.

"She was practicing when she got home, and she looked at me and said: 'B is for careful. B, careful.' "

BULLETIN BOARD ADDS: A 4-year-old girl of our acquaintance was recently making an illustrated alphabet—first printing a letter, then drawing a picture to accompany it. They all made perfect 4-year-old sense.

With H came a fireplace—for hot. With K, a shoe—for kick. With P, an indiscriminate blob with a small circle inside it.

"What's that?" we asked.

"Poop," she said.

"And what's that circle there?" we asked.

"A piece of corn," she said.

Kelly of southern Minnesota: "I was sitting in the dentist's chair, waiting for the dentist to come and give me my checkup. He was around the corner in this other cubicle with this little boy.

"The dentist was asking the little boy how school was going, and the little boy said: 'Everything's going good. I'm one of the best students in class.'

"The dentist asked him: 'Why? How come you're the best?'

"The little boy said: 'Well, I already know my ABCs. I can already tie my shoes. And I don't pick my nose like the other kids.'

"I just thought that was gross—but cute."

Barb of Como: "I remember one time when we were kids, my brother kept arguing with my mom, trying to get his way. He kept arguing and arguing, and finally she said, very emphatically: 'I said "No!" N-O, no!'

"And he said: 'Well, I said "Yes." N-S, yes!'

"I will never forget that, and neither will my mom."

Gene of St. Paul: "We have a 4-year-old daughter who is very into spelling names and printing—that type of thing. We use, as scratch paper, some of our deposit slips at the back of our check blanks. (Seems like there's always more of those left than the actual checks—but that's another story.)

"Anyway, my daughter wanted to write my name, so she asked me how to spell it—and I just pointed to the top, and I said: 'Well, there it is, right at the top.'

"After diligently working for about five minutes, she showed me, and she was really proud, and there it was—in her best penmanship: 'DEPOSIT.' "

The Jenska of River Falls, Wis.: "My daughter is in first grade this year, and she's learning to read. For a while there, she was spelling everything she saw.

"We had to stop at the cash machine one day, and she sat and spelled out: 'A-U-T-O-M-A-T-E-D T-E-L-L-E-R.'

"I said: 'That's right! What does that spell?'

"And she said: 'Bank.' "

Jen of St. Paul: "If you're an aunt or an uncle, you get really tired of hearing how smart and bright your nephews and nieces are. But I've gotta say: I was pretty impressed when I was at my sister's house and her just-turned-3-year-old, Will, came up to the table where we were unpacking a box and started spelling out: 'H-A-N-D-L-E W-I-T-H C-A-R-E.'

"But then I realized maybe he wasn't so smart as he seemed, because he turned to his mother and said: 'That spells box—right, Mom?'"

Princess Grace of Mahtomedi: "I was helping my third-grader just now with his spelling words. I say the word first, then use it in a sentence, then say it again, and then he spells it. I sometimes offer songs as a mnemonic device.

"One of the words was 'respect' today. I said 'Respect' and then started singing 'R-E-S-P-E-C-T, find out what it means to me'—and was singin', snappin' my fingers . . . when I noticed my son staring blankly at me.

"I stopped, and he disgustedly said: 'Mom, I already *know* how to spell "respect."'

"Eye-yie."

Jill of White Bear Lake: "I've got a childhood memory I'd like to share with you; it's actually for my dad, who will turn 58 on May 21st.

"The other day, as I was fertilizing my yard, I remembered back to the time when my father allowed me to fertilize his yard. I was probably about 10 years old. After he had finished explaining how to fertilize so that the grass gets evenly green, I was on my own.

"After finishing the front yard, I went to do the back yard—and the whole time I was doing the front yard, I'd kept thinking to myself: 'What a waste of time this is. These little white pebbles are not gonna do a thing for the grass.' I decided to speed things up in the back yard.

"When I'd finished, my dad was surprised that I had gotten the back yard done so fast, and he questioned me numerous times as to how I did it. All I kept replying was: 'Yes, Dad, I did the whole back yard.'

"Imagine my dad's reaction a few weeks and a lot of rain later when, looking out the top-story window down onto the back yard, he saw J-I-L-L spelled out with beautiful green grass.

"Needless to say, Dad: Yes, I do do all of my own back yard now. I love you, Dad."

Happy Mom of White Bear Lake: "Sometimes teenagers totally surprise you.

"Last night, there was a dusting of snow. This morning, when I went out to get in my car to head for work, my daughter had left the following message written in snow across my car: 'Hi, Mom. Have a good day! Love, Jodi.'

"I had a smile on my face the whole morning."

Grace of Blaine: "My mother passed away several years ago, in January, so, of course, I was feeling pretty blue. I stopped over to my son's place in Coon Rapids, and after about an hour or so, my granddaughter, Melissa, asked if I would take her sledding. I didn't really feel like it, but I said: 'OK, sure, I'll take you sledding.'

"So we get out to the car, and she says: 'Put in these two sleds.' And I thought: 'That's funny. Why does she want two sleds?' But I put 'em in the car.

"So we get over to the hill, and I take out the one sled for her, and she says: 'Grandma, take out the other sled.' And I said: 'What for?' And she said: 'For you to go down the hill.'

"That was really precious; kinda took away the gloom that I was feeling. Just a neat way for a kid to make her grandma feel better."

Happy Elf of North Oaks: "We have some friends who moved to Maryland—the most darling family—and on one holiday (I don't remember which), we sent the two boys, who were probably about 4 and 10, a gift of a set of window stickies. It was supposed to be an aquarium, with a bunch of fish.

"Well, the mom was out of town when they received them, so when she returned, the boys were very, very anxious to show them off. The elder showed off his window first and was rewarded with sufficient oohs and aahs, and then the younger led his mother to his room. And where the elder had all sorts of fishes and bubbles on his window, the little brother had gotten all the scraps of background that the fish had been punched out of.

"And he was *so* proud of it, too!"

Linda of St. Paul: "My husband and I are both artists, and we have pottery kilns and clay and things in our back yard.

"When my son was, oh, about 1½, I let him out to play in his diaper in the back yard, and he was runnin' around, and I went in and out and checked on him, and one time when I went out, right next to the door—on the house siding—was smeared the contents of his diaper.

"And I looked at it and said: 'Ohhhh, David, what is *that*?'

"To which he replied: 'Culper.'

"Took me a couple of minutes to decode it, but what he said it was was 'sculpture.' Hope this isn't a comment on our work."

Renee of Circle Pines: "Years ago, there was a new tampon on the market that expanded into a flowerlike shape when you dipped it in water.

"Don't ask me how she discovered this, but my young cousin created a *beautiful* bouquet by dipping each tampon into a cup of water dyed with food coloring.

"It really was pretty, but her teenage sister was *horrified* to discover this unique flower arrangement on the dining-room table when she brought her boyfriend home from school.

"Some people just don't appreciate artistic talent."

Beth of North St. Paul: "My brother and I used to be fascinated with the 'secret box' our mother kept in the bathroom.

"One day, my brother and the neighbor boy got ahold of the box and used the tampons in a game of Army. They unwrapped the whole boxful and used them as grenades—pulling the string and throwing them at each other.

"When my mom discovered tampons all over her yard, she was horrified! We couldn't figure out what the big deal was."

Mortimer of Eagan: "Yesterday, our 10-year-old got home from school and we were talking about what he had done during the day. He told us that Tuesday is Art Class Day for his class and that they talked about a famous painter, but he could not remember the artist's name. My wife asked if the artist was Grandma Moses.

"Our son replied in a huff: 'No, Mom, it wasn't one of your relatives.' "

Nag of El Paso, Wis.: "When my little sister, who is now 30-something, came home from the first day of first grade, she was so excited and was telling us about all of the people she met. She started talking about this one little boy who had really white hair; his eyebrows were white, and his skin was real white, and his eyes were kinda pinkish.

"My older sister said: 'Is he an albino?'

"And my little sister said: 'I'm not sure what his last name is.'"

Young **Erin** of South St. Paul: "Yesterday, while eating dinner, I said something using my first and last names.

"I asked my little sister Nikki, who's 2, what her name was. She paused and then said: 'Nikki. Nikki Honeybee'—which is my dad's nickname for her. I thought it was pretty cute."

Mama G of Apple Valley: "Last winter, my niece and her husband arrived back in Minnesota after spending several months in South Africa. (Her husband is a field-engineer-type person and gets transferred all over the world.)

"After being here only a couple of days, Mike had to return to headquarters in Chicago before going on to their next destination. My niece's daughter Becky, then 4, was distraught by the upcoming separation. As her dad was boarding the airplane, she was heard to scream: 'But Dad, I don't even know your middle name!'"

Jackie of Stillwater: "My husband had been away for a couple of days, and my little daughter, Marina, took the phone away from me and said: 'I want to give Daddy a hug.'

"She hugged the telephone with all her might and said: 'I love you, Daddy! I love you, Daddy!'

"I thought it was just the sweetest thing I ever saw."

Diane H. of Coon Rapids: "My husband regularly travels out of town—three or four days a week. I'm sitting in the kitchen this morning reading Bulletin Board, and my almost-5-year-old son yells downstairs: 'Mom, when will Dad be home?'

"I reply: 'Tomorrow.'

"And he says: 'What time?'

"I reply: 'Oh, a little bit after lunch.'

"And then, after a short pause, I hear him yell down again: 'Mom, I'm gonna have lunch at breakfast.'"

Emie Owen of White Bear Lake: "My 5-year-old son, Miles, came into our bedroom one morning, and my husband said: 'OK, Miles. Now, I'd like you to fix us some scrambled eggs and some bacon and some pancakes and some coffee and some tea.'

"Miles said: 'Why?'

"His father said: 'Well, it's your turn. We've been doing that for you all these years; it's your turn.'

"And Miles said: 'Well, I don't know. I don't know about that tea.'"

Jake's Mom of Inver Grove Heights: "Jake and I were having lunch today at McDonald's, and I looked up at the sign and it said: '98 BILLION SOLD.'

"I told him: 'Wow! Ninety-eight billion sold!' And Jake said: 'Boy, I'm surprised they haven't run out yet.'

"Pretty good for a 5-year-old."

A Homebound Mom of Vermillion: "About three weeks ago, we were driving in Apple Valley with our three children, one of whom is 6 years old. We were discussing Christmas, as we pulled up to a stoplight, when my husband said: 'Christmas is just around the corner.'

"Our 6-year-old popped his head up from the back seat and seriously asked: '*Which* corner?'"

Arlene of St. Paul: "A neighbor was backing out of the driveway and asked his 6-year-old son if there were any cars coming.

"Mikey looked both ways and said: 'Nope. No cars coming, Dad.'

"Dad backed out—and was promptly broadsided by a truck."

Reba Fan of South St. Paul: "When my sister Amanda was 4 or 5, she was learning how to cross the street safely. A friend of mine asked her, 'Why did the chicken cross the road?'—to which she promptly replied: 'Because there were no cars coming.'"

Young **Kacie** of Sunfish Lake: "My mom was doing these trivia questions with my sister Courtney—who's 5, and she loves to make people laugh.

"And you know that rhyme that goes 'Little Boy Blue, come blow your horn, the sheep's in the meadow, the cow's in the corn'? Well, the trivia question said: 'Why did Little Boy Blue blow his horn?'

"And Courtney just sort of sat there, and then she goes: 'To get attention.'"

Gloria of St. Paul: "A few weeks ago, my sister, my daughter and I were enjoying a late-summer coffee party in my back-yard gazebo. Our conversation turned to some rather intimate personal anecdotes, which provoked outbursts of uncontrollable laughter.

"That led my 11-year-old granddaughter, Michelle, to come running out of the house, wondering what was so funny.

"Well, we tried to explain that she was just too young yet to share our humor. She smiled patiently at us and said, in a rather condescending tone of voice: 'OK. I'll leave you three ladies to age gracefully.'"

Jeanne of St. Paul: "At the end of the weekly visit of grandchildren Matthew and Katie, they each take a small bag of goodies home. Usually consists of one roll, one slice of Lunds' egg-twist bread and two cookies.

"On the last visit, when we were really busy talking, we were forgetting the bags. Now, most kids would say: 'Where's my bag? Where's my bag? Where's my bag?' Matthew said, in a very grown-up manner: 'Aren't we forgetting something?'"

Carrie of Woodbury: "I was baby-sitting for two kids, ages 7 and 5. They were making birthday cards for their mom.

"The crayons they were using belonged to the 7-year-old, and she had told her brother *exactly* which crayons he was not allowed to use. He replied that he could use whatever crayons he wanted.

"She looked at me, shook her head, and—with the most disgusted voice—said: 'Kids.'"

Damma of Maplewood: "I called my daughter's house, asking to talk to Larry, my 4-year-old grandson—who at the time was watching a movie and apparently did not want to be interrupted.

"Reluctantly, he came to the phone—and, when hearing my

voice, he immediately disguised *his* voice, saying: 'There's no Larry here. You've got a wrong number'—and disconnected me."

Grandma DeDe of Woodbury: "I got a phone call this morning from my little Benny, who is 5. Usually on Wednesday mornings, I take care of him while his mother bowls.

"Well, he called this morning—and he said: 'Grandma? If I go to Sam's house today, I hurt you?'

"I said: 'No, Benny. You won't hurt me. You just go play at Sam's, and have a good time.'

"I thought it was sweet. He didn't want to hurt my feelings by not coming over. Pretty nice little 5-year-old, don't you think?

"He's always doing nice little things. The other day, I was taking care of him—and he really was a mess, and I said: 'You go clean up before lunch, Benny.'

"And when he reappeared, he was barefooted, had his brother's too-big pants on, a sport coat that was two sizes too small, a white shirt and a bow tie.

"He looked at me with a cute little smile, and he said: 'Grandma? I look good enough for lunch?'

"Well, he looked like Charlie Chaplin, but I told him he looked just like a bridegroom—and he did. He's a gorgeous little boy."

Rob of the East Side: "I've got a 3½-year-old granddaughter, and she's finally understanding that I'm her mother's father. We were sittin' here talking the other day, and I said: 'You know, I remember when your mommy was a little girl, just like you.'

"Well, it was a short time later that she got mad at her mom about something. She says: 'You're mean!' She starts dialing away, and she says: 'I'm callin' the police.'

"And she looked at me, and she says: 'Your little girl's goin' to jail!'"

Becca of Mahtomedi (echoed by **Leigh** of Mahtomedi, who must have been there, too): "I'm here at my church. I just got done helping out with a Sunday-school class. We were asking the kids what the source of love is, and we were intending for them to say, you know, whatever you hold as the Supreme Being. And this one little girl said: 'Money.'

"The next question we asked was: 'What is something that you need every day?' And we were hoping the kids were gonna say food and water and shelter and stuff—and one kid said: 'Lawyers.' These are 5-year-olds!

"Kinda scared me a little bit. Scary morning at church."

Peggy of St. Paul: "My friend Loretta and her little girl were driving in the car one day, and they drove past the Cathedral.

"Her little girl said: 'Mom, look! There's God's house!'

"And Loretta said: 'Yes, honey, that *is* God's house.'

"And her little girl said: 'How come when we're in God's house, we never see God?'

"And Loretta said: 'Well, honey, that's because God's in everyone. There's a little piece of God in everyone. That's why when you meet people, you should always be nice to them, even if they're not really nice to you back—because there's a little piece of God in everyone.'

"Her daughter started thinking about it, and Loretta was thinking: 'That sounded pretty *good!*'

"Her daughter's thinking about it, and she looks at her mom and says: 'Mom, do I have his head?'"

Kiwi of Afton: "Today, I was at my littlest cousin Maria's baptism.

"While sitting there, Maria's older sister Lauren, who'll be 5 on Thursday, asked our grandma where God was.

"Grandma said: 'God is all around us, and this is one of his many houses.'

"Lauren looked around the church and replied: 'Then where's his kitchen?'"

Gene of parts unknown: "Years ago, I was sitting in a lawn chair in the back yard, reading my paper, when my daughter came up to me and said, 'Dad, does Jesus live in the whole sky?'

"And I was concentrating on the paper, and I said, absentmindedly, 'I think so.'

"And she said, 'Boy, there must be a lot of furniture.'"

Laurie of Prescott, Wis.: "My 4-year-old daughter, Chelsea, and I were driving home the other day after I'd picked her up from day care, and she was looking out the window—pondering the way 4-year-olds do. She turned to me, and she said: 'Mom, is God up in the sky?'

"I said: 'Yeah, Chelse, God's up in the sky.' And then about a minute later, she looked at me and she goes: 'Do you think she's nice?'

"I said: 'Chelse, I'm sure she is.'

"This is a kid you could really love."

Grandma Shirley of Maplewood: "Yesterday, my grandson Christopher and I were sitting watching the storm, and he was talking about the thunder being God bowling and the lightning being the angels playing with flashlights.

"He said: 'Grandma, who's making it rain?'

"And I said: 'Well, Christopher, I think God is.'

"And he said: 'No, Grandma. God can't be doin' that, 'cause he's in charge of bowling.'

"So I said: 'Well, maybe Jesus is the one making it rain.'

"He looked at me, and he said: 'Yep. You know, Grandma, that does make sense.'"

Flyer of South St. Paul: "About 10 years ago, I was with my daughter out in a boat on Lake Miltona in Alexandria, and there was this incredible, incredible sunset.

"We were staring at it for a while, and my daughter—who was 3 or 4 at the time—said: 'Gee, Dad, it looks just like Jesus takin' off.'

"And I thought: It sure does."

Grandma Gerry of Red Wing: "My granddaughters Kacie and Kelsey were at my house one day—and, while looking at a map, Kacie says: 'Grandma, where's La Crosse?'

"Before I had a chance to reply, Kelsey says: 'Isn't that where Jesus died?'"

Bo 6 of Shoreview: "When our son was about 5, we were all in church . . . and this was at the time when 'The Dukes of Hazzard' was popular, and he was quietly playing with his General Lee car.

"We didn't think he was paying much attention, but apparently he had one ear open, because the priest made reference to 'Jesus of

Nazareth,' and he suddenly looked up, his eyes wide open; his mouth fell open, and he exclaimed—loud enough for five rows to hear: 'I didn't know there was a *Jesus* of Hazzard!'"

Megan J. Thomas of St. Paul: "My mother had taken my god-niece to church with her one morning, and everything was going pretty well when Jessica leaned over and asked, in a stage whisper: 'Grandma, why is everyone talking about God?'

"The preacher must have wondered why three rows of parish-ioners cracked up."

Auntie Mame of St. Paul: "On Christmas Eve, I was sitting in church next to my 6-year-old nephew, Matthew, and during a break in the action, I leaned over and said: 'I really hope you like what I got you for Christmas, Matt.'

"And he, being a very well-brought-up little boy, said: 'I'm sure I will.' And then, under his breath, I heard him say: 'I just hope it's not a *Barbie doll*.'"

Brian of Forest Lake: "I just got home from church. It was nearing the end of the sermon when my 4-year-old son, Benjamin, whispered something to me. I thought maybe he was seeking some fatherly advice. I didn't catch it the first time, so I asked him to say it again.

"He whispered: 'When are the Publishers' Clearinghouse guys coming?'"

Pat of St. Paul: "I walked in the door the other day, and my kids were all excited. They said: 'Mom! Mom! You're a finalist! You're a finalist in the Publishers' Clearinghouse sweepstakes!'

"And then they looked at me, smiled real big and said: 'We're gonna *make* it—'cause Dad is a finalist, too.'"

Lou of West St. Paul: "I'm Catholic, and our kids hear us praying around the house, and I'll never forget the day when one of my little kids decided that he wanted to pray with us. He came out with the following prayer: 'Hail, Mary, full of grease, the Lord is with me. Blessed are you among women, and blessed is Fruit-of-the-Loom Jesus.'

"I really don't remember the rest of what he said, because I was laughing too hard at that point in the game."

Mike of Stillwater, telling a story about his little brother: "About the only person of color he had ever seen was my sister, who was adopted from India.

"One Sunday, my parents decided to take us kids out of suburbia to a church in downtown Minneapolis. About 95 percent of the people there were black, and my brother leaned over to my mom and asked her: 'Why are there so many adopted people here?'"

Mike of Red Wing: "Last Sunday, my daughter and I were in church when, about halfway through the service, she asked if she could switch places with me.

"As I moved over, I realized she had been behind a fairly tall man who must have been blocking her view.

"As she moved, she exclaimed: 'I can see! It's a miracle!'"

BULLETIN BOARD REPLIES: You've reminded us of one of our favorite bits by Father (later Monsignor) Guido Sarducci of "Saturday Night Live"—in which he railed against the Catholic Church's discrimination against Italians in its conferring of official sainthoods.

Sarducci alleged that the American saints had been credited with far fewer miracles than many, many Italians still on the waiting list—and that, furthermore, some of the American saints' miracles had been card tricks.

Megan's Mom of Chetek, Wis.: "My daughter, who just turned 5, loves to play Old Maid with her grandma.

"Her grandma remarked to me to other day that she is amazed how Megan *always* wins. She was wondering if Megan somehow marked the back of the cards.

"I turned to Megan and said: 'Honey, you don't cheat when you play cards with Grandma, do you?'

"Her reply: 'No! I can see Grandma's cards in her glasses.'"

BULLETIN BOARD REPLIES: And the girl's right: That's not cheating.

Ask any cardsharp.

Kris, Mom of 2 of Stillwater: "My son Benjamin, who is 6, was really into the Olympics. He recognized the U.S. athletes, and he'd cheer 'em on. He even seemed to understand what scores were good for the figure skaters. I was really quite impressed.

"We were watching downhill racing, and he knew the skiers had to go around the flags. And a U.S. skier was racing down the hill, and Benjamin jumped up and yelled: 'Take a shortcut! Take a shortcut!' He sat down, looked at me and said: 'You know, Mom, he'd go faster if he took a shortcut.'

"Maybe he didn't understand as well as I thought he had."

Julie of Roseville: "I was in Florida last year, playin' on the beach, and a couple of really cute kids from South Carolina were playin' in the sand by us, and one of them was pointing out in the ocean, and there was an orange buoy that the lifeguard swims around.

"He looks and he points and says: 'What's thaaaaat?'

"And I go: 'That's a buoy.'

"And he says, in his little accent: 'Is that his haid?' "

Petronella: "Our 18-month-old boy imitates everything we do, which is cute and horrifying all at once.

"The Cute One took my husband's razor off the counter, took the cap off and tried to 'shave' his face. I got it away from him right away.

"At 5 A.M. the next morning, we were rushing to get ready for work, and my husband starts laughing hysterically. 'Look,' he says, showing me the razor. There were little tiny, fuzzy, blond hairs on the razor from The Cute One.

"By the way, The Cute One can say the words 'chicken,' 'duck,' and 'piggie'—but he can't say 'Mama.' "

K.T. of Lexington: "We all expect our kids to say their first words, such as 'mama,' 'dada'—all that good stuff. And my son of a year comes out with 'Oh, pewie!'

"He runs around the house smelling his feet all the time and saying 'Oh, pewie!' "

Merlyn of St. Paul: "I grew up spending a lot of time with my family, including a lot of cousins.

"We were all camping in Chippewa Falls for a weekend one time, and we big kids decided to watch a baseball game across the road. My little cousin Bob tagged along. He was a silent kid; I had never heard him say a word—and did think something might be wrong with him.

"As we climbed the bleachers, someone stepped on him, and out of his mouth came: 'Ouch! You're stepping on my hand!'

"Everybody stopped dead. 'What did he say? Bob, say it again!' Nothing.

"A few minutes later, as we sat in the stands, we were passing around someone's sunglasses and putting them on and laughing when a little voice from between the seats said: 'May I try them on?' You guessed it: Bob—again.

"It seems he never spoke unless it was absolutely necessary—and then only in full sentences. In a talkative family like mine, this concept was beyond our grasp.

"When I got older and took jobs teaching, I wished I had a classroom *full* of Bobs."

Marian the Librarian of Menomonie, Wis.: "My 2-year-old son, Joshua, never used more than a word or two at a time, and we were getting concerned that his speech might not be developing at the rate that it should be.

"I guess his ears were making up for it, because one morning, as we prepared to drive his two older sisters to school, he uttered his first almost-sentence: 'My turn front seat now, Mommy.'

"I love you, Josh."

Leslie of parts undisclosed: "I don't recall my brother's first words, but I do recall his most confusing words.

"In the late '60s, when he was about 2 years old, he used to pop up from behind chairs or peek around corners and such and say: *'Seedy enk-el-a-sing.'* He'd say this over and over, each time laughing like crazy.

"For days and weeks, he said this—*Seedy enk-el-a-sing*—and then he'd laugh.

"We tried everything we could to get him to speak more distinctly: 'What?!' 'Slow down!' 'Say that again!'

"To no avail. Nothing worked.

"Finally, one Monday night we were all sitting around the television watching 'Laugh-In,' and up from behind a bush popped Arte Johnson in his German uniform saying: 'Verrrry interesting.'

"My brother laughed along with the soundtrack and shouted: *'Seedy enk-el-a-sing! Seedy enk-el-a-sing!'* "

M. of Inver Grove Heights: "Here's another story of a kid who probably watched too much TV:

"When my son was 4 years old, he and my husband were saying evening prayers by the bedside. My husband went on for some time, giving thanks and asking for guidance, and when he finally said 'Amen,' my son gave a sigh and said: 'That's it—and now it's good night, for NBC News.' "

K. of Maplewood: "I've just gotten over some medical problems that caused my husband and me to think about what would happen if one or both of us died. We went over our life insurance, and we talked about our choice of a guardian for our children.

"Thinking that our kids were old enough to be part of this decision, I asked my 10-year-old son: 'If something happened to Daddy and me, and you had to go live with someone else, would you rather live with Lynn—she's a friend of our family—or your Uncle Tom?'

"My son got very serious, and then he asked: 'Which one has cable?' "

Charly of St. Paul: "My husband and I have been noting that our soon-to-be-13-year-old son has been undergoing quite a few changes—the most obvious being the physical ones.

"The other day, after he took a shower, I called my son back into the bathroom to pick up after himself. This usually quite modest boy came rushing in naked, scooped up his underwear—and as he raced back out, he called: 'Don't look down, Mom!'

"I said: 'Hey, I'm your mom! You don't have anything I haven't seen before.'

"To which he replied: 'Yeah, Mom, but now it's new and improved!' "

Sarah of Eagan: "About 10 years ago, I went to Denver to visit my oldest daughter and her family. My granddaughter, Bridget, was about 5 at the time. Since my daughter and her husband both would be working, I offered to baby-sit Bridget.

"After we were up, fed, dressed and ready for the day, I asked her what we should do. She suggested we go see the latest kids' movie that was being advertised on TV.

"I said: 'Honey, I don't know where it's playing.'

"Her exasperated response to her dumb grandmother: 'Well, Grandma, it's at a theater near you!'"

Mary of St. Paul: "One day, my nephew Joey was playing with a neighbor friend in the yard, and my brother-in-law came out and said it was time for his friend to go. So Joe took his friend's hand and started walking over to his little friend's house.

"My brother-in-law asked: 'Where are you going, Joe? You have to come inside now.'

"He turned to my brother-in-law and said: 'Don't worry, Dad. I'll be right back after these messages.'

"Isn't that cute?"

Barb of Maple Grove: "I received my *Smithsonian* for January yesterday, and I was looking at it, and my 2½-year-old son came up—and on the back cover is an ad for Colombian coffee, and there's a picture of three polar bears on it.

"My son came up to me and said: 'I know what those are. Those are polar bear.' And without missing a beat, he said: 'They dwink Coke.'"

Karen Hanson of Pine Island: "Some of our grandsons were spending the weekend. A TV ad for a 'monster' truck show had them talking about what they would drive—someday.

"The 13-year-old will have a Dodge Ram. The 9-year-old wants a Chevy. The 6-year-old said: 'I'm going to drive a Ford Lately!'

"Enjoy the Bulletin Board greatly!"

BULLETIN BOARD REPLIES: The lady is a poet.

Jerry of South Minneapolis: "Last summer, I flew to the Carolinas to visit some good friends, and on the plane, I had three young kids seated behind me. After takeoff, I heard them squealing with excitement.

"The first one said: 'I feel like a roller coaster.'

"Another half-laughed with: 'I feel weird.'

"And the third, a little girl, jumped in with 'I feel like Chicken Tonight.'

"I burst out laughing; I still laugh whenever I see it on TV."

Jen of Eagan: "My 4-year-old daughter and I were watching 'Lovejoy,' and I was explaining about the car being English, with the driver on the right—and that the car itself was a VW Bug convertible. My daughter couldn't see what the car looked like completely, so she got up, walked over to the TV and tried to look down into the TV to see what the rest of the car looked like."

Michelle of Cottage Grove: "My 2-year-old is sitting here watching *One Hundred and One Dalmatians*, for the umpteenth time, and she decided to go over to her play phone and call Cruella De Vil.

"She picks it up and says: 'Cruella, *please* don't take the puppies.'"

Barb of Eagan: "I was just putting my 7-year-old son to bed. Earlier in the evening, we had made a deal that he could have a friend over this evening if he would not set his alarm to get up early to watch cartoons—because he would be going to bed later than usual. We agreed.

"But tonight, when I was putting him to bed, he wanted to set his alarm, and I reminded him of our deal. He said: 'God, can you please rewind the world so I can make that deal over again?'

"Interesting concept."

A.L. of St. Paul: "When my daughter was about 5 years old, she used to come downstairs every morning and always tell me about her dreams. Never failed. Every morning.

"One morning, she comes down and says: 'Mom, I didn't have any dreams last night. I must have run out of film.'"

Mark of the West Side: "This is a story of a 3-year-old daughter, having been roused from her nap and rubbing her eyes very tiredly.

"I asked her: 'How come you're awake? You're supposed to be sleeping.'

"She looked at me with a real sad look on her face and said: 'I ran out of dreams.'"

Grandma Marge of the East Side: "After I had washed my youngest son Johnny's pillow, he was extremely upset. When I asked him why, he said: 'You washed all the good dreams out of it.'"

Anvil of Merriam Park: "Me and the kids were sitting around watching *Snow White* the other day—and at the part where she's kneeling down to give her little evening prayer and she wishes for all of her dreams to come true, my almost-8-year-old chimes in and says: 'No! She can't do that! What if she has a bad dream?'"

C.P. of St. Paul: "I have a 4-year-old, and he was playing with his trucks one Saturday morning, and my husband and I were sitting there drinking coffee, and I said: 'Kyle, you've gotta quit coming into our room in the middle of the night, because you're kicking me in the back.'

"He said: 'Oh, OK.'

"And I said: 'Why did you come in, anyways?'

"And he said: 'I had a bad dream.'

"And I said: 'A bad dream? What'd you dream about?'

"And he looks up at me and goes: 'You!'"

Bobbie of Farmington: "Last night, my almost 3-year-old, Ernestine, came in at about 3 in the morning and started telling Daddy about how Mommy's arms were caught in the door of a choo-choo train. She wasn't really sad, just kind of concerned, and he told her: 'No, honey. Mommy's right here. Mommy's arms are fine.'

"I was kind of half-asleep; he picked up my arms and showed her my arms were fine.

"Ernestine kept saying: 'No, Mommy's arms are in the choo-choo train! The choo-choo train's door closed on Mommy's arms! Mommy's arms are in the choo-choo train!' He kept trying to tell her my arms were fine.

"So finally we let her crawl up in bed with us, and she wouldn't go to sleep until she could hold my arms for the rest of the night.

"It was so cute. Every time I'd try to roll over, she'd reach back over and pull my arms, and said that she didn't want Mommy's arms to be broken; she wanted to make sure that my arms were OK.

"She's my oldest, and it's the first time she's been able to tell me what kind of bad dreams she has."

Marjorie of White Bear Lake: "My 6-year-old granddaughter, Caylee Jo, came into the house from the garage carrying a bedraggled tennis racquet.

" 'Can I have this to sleep with?' she asked her mother.

" 'What do you want to sleep with that dirty old thing for?' her mother asked.

" 'I just want it. Can't I have it? Please!'—and the exchange went on for a few minutes, before her mother, rather reluctantly, gave in. (Caylee can be very persistent.)

"Caylee was overjoyed and headed for the stairs. As she climbed the stairs to her room, her mother overheard her say: 'Boy, is this ever going to make a great dream catcher!' Caylee has the tennis racquet handle wedged down between the mattress and the headboard of her bed, with the 'ratty' end standing up to catch any wonderful dreams that might happen by."

Anonymous woman: "One time when my son was 12, my husband and I were sitting in the living room—nothing particular was going on—when he walked in the room and said: 'I must have had a wet dream last night.' Just came out with it, right like that.

"I looked over at my husband, and I thought he'd turned to stone. The Kool-Aid he was drinking—he had the glass halfway up to his mouth, and it was just kinda *frozen* there.

"Very calmly, I asked: 'Well, honey, what do you mean?'

"And he said: 'I peed in the bed—so it must have been a wet dream.'

"I sent him upstairs, and then my husband and I laughed ourselves silly.

"And then he asked me: 'Well, are *you* gonna tell him?'

"I said: 'Hell, no. Are *you* gonna tell him?'

"Now he's 14, and I guess nobody needs to tell him anymore."

Grama H. of Maplewood: "Our 4-year-old granddaughter, Kellie, was watching with interest as our daughter nursed our new grandson. She said: 'Mommy, why is K.C. biting you there?'

"Our daughter replied: 'Mommies get milk in their breasts to feed babies.'

"Kellie turned and started to walk away, then turned around suddenly, lifted up her shirt and said: 'Look, Mom, I got Kool-Aid!'"

June of North St. Paul: "My daughter came down from the far-northwest corner of North Dakota for a visit and stopped to see her 3½-year-old niece/godchild, Krista. She hadn't seen her for a year, and she says: 'My goodness, but you're getting big! How'd you get so big?'

"And very seriously, Krista looked at her and said: 'I drink Kool-Aid.'"

Patty of St. Paul: "I had the stomach flu this winter, and I was lying in bed, trying not to move, when my 7-year-old came and asked me if he could help me.

"I said: 'Yes, David. Could you take this cup of 7-Up?' (It was a cup with a little cover on it.) I said: 'I can't drink it. I want water, instead. Very carefully take it, and dump it out, and fill it with cold water.' And he did that—and God bless him, he didn't spill any.

"I had some, and it tasted much better. I wanted to encourage such good behavior, so I praised him and told him what a good helper he was.

"He started to walk away, and then he turned at the doorway—and looking very important, he said: 'If you need any farther refillments, just call for me.'

"And I said: 'Thank you, David.' And I laughed.

"It was so cute: 'If you need any farther refillments, just call for me.' I wrote it down; I mean, I was so sick I could hardly move, but I pulled a pencil out of the night stand and wrote down his exact words."

Kamy of the East Side: "I was suddenly ill with the flu, and I lay down on the couch and went to sleep *immediately*.

"It must have been about a half an hour later when I wake up, and my son Tom, who was about 3 years old, is standing there in front of me with a big glass of water. He says: 'This is for you, Mommy.' So I was really grateful for the water, and I drink it down and go back to sleep.

"About another half hour goes by, and the same thing: I wake up, and he's standing in front of me with more water—only now I'm awake enough to think: Tom's been scolded a couple times lately for climbing up on the cupboards in the kitchen to reach the sink, so I ask: 'Did you climb on the counter?'

"And he says: 'Oh, no, Mommy'—and he's smiling real proudly. He says: 'I know I'm not supposed to do that, so I got your water from the toilet.'"

Gypsy of South St. Paul: "My husband and I were talking tonight, and he said that when he was little—about 2 or 3 years old—his mom wouldn't let him have water before he went to bed. And he knew that if he got up, she would hear the faucet when he turned it on. So he pulled the head off of this doll; it was a big head, and he'd stick it in the toilet and fill the head up with water and drink out of that.

"I thought it was really cute. Kinda sick, but really cute."

L.A. of Cottage Grove: "I had the distinctly unpleasant task yesterday of removing a splinter from my 6-year-old son's knee. It had gotten infected, and we just couldn't let it go anymore. This, of course, involved a needle and some antiseptic that stung.

"He was crying; I felt terrible that I had to do this to him and inflict this pain.

"I felt much better at dinner, however, when he said: 'Mom, you really love us, don't you?'

"I said: 'Well yes, of course I do.'

"And he said: 'I knew that because you always want to kill our bacteria.'"

Becky of Cottage Grove: "When my daughter was about 4 years old, we were out camping. She was walking around barefoot, and all of a sudden she started screeching. She came running to me, and she had a *huge* sliver in her foot.

"I went down to pull out the sliver, and she started screaming; she didn't want me to touch it. I was sweet-talking her: 'Oh, come on. It won't be that bad.' She screamed and screamed and wouldn't let me near it.

"Finally, we even tried holding her down, but she became just like a little wild animal; there was just no way we could do it.

"So after a while, we all got tired, and she decided that she was gonna lie down for a nap in the camper. While she was sleeping, I reached in and pulled out the sliver from her foot.

"When she woke up, I said: 'Honey, do you know what I did when you were sleeping?' She said: 'No.' And I said: 'Well, I pulled the sliver out of your foot.'

"Her eyes got big, and she started smiling, and I said: 'You know, it couldn't have hurt that much, because you didn't even wake up when I pulled that sliver out.' She smiled even harder, and I said: 'So what are you gonna do the next time you have a sliver in your foot?'

"She said: 'I'm gonna go straight to bed.'"

Kelly of St. Paul: "We were at a restaurant the other day—and I'm not gonna say the name of it, because normally they serve really good food—but we were with a friend of mine's son, who is 8 years old, and he ordered a grilled-cheese sandwich, and he got the sandwich, and it was Velveeta, which we all know is disgusting.

"He looked at it, took a bite out of it, and he didn't like it—and all of a sudden, he was gone! Half the sandwich was gone, too.

"So his father followed him, into the bathroom, and the 8-year-old, Sean, went into one of the stalls, and didn't lock the door—and his dad came in, and half the sandwich was in the toilet, and the kid was *peeing* on it!

"His dad gave him a talking-to, and he said: 'So what lesson have you learned today?'

"And Sean says: 'I better lock the door.'"

Susan of White Bear Township: "I'm a toddler teacher, and we're in the process of toilet-training one of our little 2½-year-old boys.

"We were out on the playground, and he said: 'Susie, I have to go potty.' So inside we went—and halfway in, I realized that he wasn't going to make it. He had poop all the way down his sweatpants.

"So I took him into the bathroom and helped him get all cleaned up. He got his shoes and his socks off, so he could take off his sweatpants and his little underpants.

"Got a fresh pair of underpants and some shorts on. He was getting his shoes and his socks back on, and he looked at me and he said: 'Susie, I'm *so* happy that I didn't poop in my socks.'

"I just had to laugh."

A Grandma of White Bear Lake: "I was taking care of my little 5-year-old granddaughter, Lindsey, the other night, and she came running into the bathroom while I was fixing my hair, and she had to go very bad, and she was so happy that she'd made it.

"I said: 'Aren't we lucky to have a toilet in the house? When Grandma was little, we only had toilets outside.'

"And she said: 'Oh, you mean Satellites?'"

Marge of Mahtomedi: "While winding my way around and around up the parking ramp, searching for a space, I said to my 3-year-old grandson, Danny: 'We're going around in circles, aren't we?'

"His response was: 'No, Grandma, we're going around in rectangles.'"

Jenna's Mom of Woodbury: "Last night, my 4-year-old daughter was in her pajamas, all clean and cozy and getting ready for her bedtime story. I kissed the top of her head and hugged her as she sat on my lap.

"I said: 'Jenna, I love you so much there just aren't words to describe it.'

"And she answered: 'How 'bout infinity, Mom?'"

T.L. of Hutchinson: "During long car trips, the kids invariably asked: 'Are we almost there yet?'

"The father of these kids came up with what he thought was a bulletproof means to end this: 'I don't want you to ask "Are we almost there yet?"—because we won't get there until after dark.'

"Victory appeared at hand, until one of the tykes quipped: 'Is it almost dark yet?'"

Anderkid of St. Paul: "One day in the Early Childhood Family Education class I go to with my 1½-year-old, Carolyn, the teacher was going over a song about putting on mittens: 'Thumb in the thumb place, fingers all together.'

"She stopped and asked: 'Does anyone know how to put your thumb in the thumb place?'

"And Carolyn promptly popped her thumb into her mouth. She knew where that thumb belonged. She even put her other fingers together—just as the teacher had demonstrated."

Overmatched of Cottage Grove: "My granddaughter Abby was 3½ years old and an earnest thumb-sucker. She had just begun attending preschool, and her parents had been using the fact that she was now a big girl and went to school to stop the thumb-sucking.

"Abby was visiting Grandma and me on a Saturday. I noticed that she was sucking her thumb. I said: 'Abby, I thought you were a big girl now that you go to school—and that you didn't suck your thumb.'

"Abby replied: 'There are school days, and there are sucking days. Today is a sucking day.'

"We expect that someday Abby will run for political office."

Gloria of the West Side: "Yesterday, our 2½-year-old son was deprived of a Popsicle for not eating his dinner. As he watched his sister eat hers, he turned to me and said: 'Mom, how 'bout I should lick it, not eat it—OK?'

"We had to laugh—and wonder if we have a future president on our hands."

Timmy of St. Paul: "Last night, two of my married friends came over with their 4-year-old and 6-month-old children. To keep the 4-year-old happy, I put in one of my Bugs Bunny videocassettes. When the cassette ended and started rewinding, the regular program came on—an interview with Senator Ted Kennedy.

"Brendon looked at old Teddy and asked: 'What cartoon is this?'

"Pretty perceptive for a 4-year-old, I thought."

Mary of Stillwater: "You think grownups have troubles and concerns? My 7-year-old just told me she's worried that the president will drive up and ask for her while she's taking a shower.

"How would you like *that* hanging over your head?"

Scott of Cottage Grove: "Two years ago, my son—then 4 years old; his name is David—got a Kit Kat candy bar as a Halloween treat. A Kit Kat has four sections to it, and he and I agreed that we would share this candy bar 50/50—or two sections apiece.

"He opened up the candy bar, broke off one section, handed it to me and said: 'There you go, Dad. There's your part.'

"I said: 'Well, wait a minute, David. I thought we were gonna divide it in half.'

"And he very honestly looked at me and said, 'You're right'—and reached out, took the one piece that he gave to me, snapped it in half, and returned it to me.

"He said: 'There you go, Dad. There's your half.'"

Mom of Six of Hastings: "Last night, my sister, who's a teacher, was doing some kindergarten-readiness skills with my 4½-year-old. She went through some simple addition—like 2 plus 1 is 3—and he got those all right. Then she said: 'Well, let's do some take-aways now.'

"In all seriousness, he looked at her and said: 'We don't *do* take-aways at my house. We *share* our toys.'"

The Dairy Girl of Hastings: "A while ago, I was baby-sitting a 4-year-old and a 7-year-old, and when I asked the 4-year-old why his mom took his dad's car to work and his dad took his mom's car, he looked at me and said: 'It's called . . . sharing.'"

Mom of Highland Park: "Can't believe I'm calling in this story, but I've laughed about it all day, so I thought I would go ahead and call it in:

"Last night in the middle of the night—about 3 o'clock—one of my kids got me up. Needed something, and after I finished with him, I went into the bathroom and sat down—and expelled a little gas.

"And I hear, from an adjacent bedroom, my son yelling: 'Mom, I can smell your toot from here!'

"All I could think was: 'Thank you for sharing.'

"All I said was: 'Go . . . to . . . sleep.'"

Laura of St. Paul: "Strange requests:

"We were camping last weekend, and I was laying down in the tent with our 2-year-old when I accidentally let out a little . . . toot. Or a . . . you know.

"He looked at me and said: 'Do it *again*, Mama!'"

Bob's Wife of Woodbury: "In our house, we have a small space between the living room and the dining room where our 2-year-old daughter likes to play. She was there yesterday, when—unbeknownst to me—she was listening to the conversation I was having with her father.

"I was saying to him: 'I have to go out. I'm going crazy. I have to go somewhere—go on the patio, go to the store, go to the end of the driveway. I don't care, but I have to go *somewhere*.'

"That was when my daughter looked up, with all her 2-year-old charm, and said, helpfully: 'Go potty, Mommy!'

"Not exactly what I had in mind."

Shirley of St. Paul: "I'm waiting to adopt, so I don't have a child yet, but I do have a niece whom I just adore. The other day, I went to pick her up with our truck. I had taken our black Lab along, and I had her in the back of the truck. I said to my niece, when I went in the house: 'Guess who's waiting in the truck for you!'

"She said: 'I dunno.' And I said: 'I'll give you a hint. She has four legs.'

"She looked at me and said: 'Grandma?'

"Isn't that the cutest thing?"

Mary of Maplewood: "I took our son Joey, who is 9, to Perkins for brunch after a hockey tournament this weekend. We have five children and don't take the kids out for meals very often, as it would cost a small fortune to feed us all.

"Anyway, we were sitting there and Joey says: 'I sure do like going to these fancy restaurants.' I just smiled and nodded.

"A little while later, he was messing around with the shrimp he had ordered and said: 'Boy! Wouldn't you think at a nice place like this, they would at least take the tails off the shrimp?'

"I had to laugh out loud."

Bambino of St. Paul: "When my older boy was 5, we were eating at Red Lobster, and he wanted to know when he could order one of those live lobsters swimmin' around there. I told him that on his 10th birthday, we'd take him there and he could do that.

"After he got over his initial excitement, he turned to me and said: 'And you know, Dad, if you're still alive then, you can come, too!'"

A.W. of St. Paul: "I have a little 6-year-old cousin named Carl, and he has this strange obsession with how old everyone else will be when he's 15.

"My grandparents came up to visit, and they're pretty old, and Carl goes to my grandpa: 'How old will you be when I'm 15 . . . Oh, wait! Are you gonna be *alive* when I'm 15?'"

Joanne of Pine City: "My granddaughter was 5 years old on January 31, and my husband and I took her out for lunch. She said to me: 'When I grow up and have my children, my mother will be a grandmother!'

"I looked at her, and I said: 'Well, that's nice, Katie. What'll I be?'

"And she said: 'Dead.'"

Ace of Wyoming: "My now-collegiate daughter, Erika, had a unique way to deal with her grandfather's death. He died at quite an early age, 58, and she had only seen him in photographs.

"As a 3-year-old with quite a command of the English language, upon browsing through the family album, she spotted Grandpa Jack, looked us right in the eyes, made an X with her finger over the picture and said: 'Well, we can cross *him* off.'

"I don't know where that came from, and Erika still can't believe she said it."

Hastings Mom of Six: "We were at the supper table last night, talking about the planets, and my son said something about wanting to see Mars in the sky, and my 5-year-old said: 'I saw Great-grandma in the sky the other day.'

"His great-grandmother died last spring. I said: 'You saw Great-grandma?'

"And he said: 'Yeah.'

"And I said: 'Well, Micah, what did she say to you?'

"And he looked at me, and he said: 'She didn't say *anything*, Mom. She's *dead!*'"

Bernie of St. Paul: "When my son was 4 years old, we had a bad car accident in which my mother-in-law was killed. I was in the hospital, and so was my son, with multiple fractures. He was on the floor below me, and lonesome, so the superintendent brought him up to my bed.

"He wanted to know where Gramma was.

"I said: 'She isn't here anymore.'

"He said: 'Where *is* she?'

"So I said: 'Up in the sky.' (Clever?)

"A big silence, and then he said: 'Uh-huh.'

"So I asked him: 'Uh-huh what?'

"And he answered: 'I think I see her feet.'"

Annette of St. Paul: "My boss' son, David, is 5 years old. David attended his first funeral last Saturday with his family. I saw David on Sunday and asked him what he thought of it.

"His answer: 'She was already dead when we got there.'"

Maureen of White Bear Lake: "A couple weeks ago, my in-laws were watching my 4-year-old daughter while my husband and I were at work, and when they got here, they told me that they had to take her to a funeral.

"My older daughter, who's 7, was complaining that she never gets to go to a funeral: Why does her little sister always get to go to funerals, but she doesn't?

"I had to explain to her that in order for her to be able to go to a funeral, somebody we know and love would have to die, and we'd miss 'em, and funerals aren't really that fun to go to; we go to 'em out of respect.

"So later that night, around the dinner table, I was asking my girls how their day was, and my older daughter had asked my younger daughter: 'How was the funeral today, Jess?'

"Jess looked at her and said: 'Ah, it was just some dead guy in a box.'"

Proud Grandma Wanda of West St. Paul: "My 2-year-old grandson, Evan, his mom and dad went to a wake last night to pay their respects to a relative's father. While they were standing by the coffin saying a prayer, Evan looked at the deceased, then waved his little hand and said softly: 'Night-night.'

"This brought tears to everyone's eyes—even mine now, as I tell about it."

Shirley of Ridgeland, Wis.: "I read your story about the small child saying 'Night-night' to a body at the funeral home. It reminded me of my own small daughter.

"We took her to view the body of her great-grandmother, and she asked: 'Why did they put Great-grandma in a jewelry box?'"

Angie Nelson of Roseville: "Our grandson Jason was trying to recall what his great-grandmother, who passed away a couple years ago, looked like. He asked his mom, and she said: 'Well, she walked with a cane and had thick glasses and white hair.'

"Jason looked bright-eyed and said: 'Oh, yeah, I remember! And she had ruffles on her face, too!'"

Sara of St. Paul: "We were just going into the cemetery this past Memorial Day, and my mother was kind of bummed out. She looked at my 4-year-old son, Ryan, and said: 'Do you remember what Grandpa looked like?'

"Ryan went: 'He has glasses.' And we went: 'Yeah.'

"And he said: 'He's got gray hair.' And we went: 'Yeah, that sounds like Grandpa.'

"And he goes: 'He has two eyes . . . a nose . . . a mouth . . . and a penis.'

"Well, it just broke us all up; we all started laughing. It made the whole afternoon lighter, 'cause it's a kinda sad thing, going to the cemetery. We told him that if Grandpa was alive, he'd laugh at that one, too."

Ol' Virginny of Cottage Grove: "When we sat down to supper on the day my son Edward was buried, my 4-year-old grandson Burt said grace. Then he said 'Amen,' paused for a second, and said, poetically: 'And as for Ed, he's dead.'

"The silence was so loud you could almost hear it."

Tracy of Apple Valley: "Just last night, our friend Cindy came to visit us. She had just returned from a trip to California, where she had a fairly lengthy stay at her father's deathbed.

"She was relating to my 5-year-old daughter a carefully worded version of her father's death. Through it all, my 5-year-old sat very intently and listened.

"At the end of the story, my friend said to her: 'Caitlin, do you know what the hardest part of the whole funeral was for me?'"

"And my daughter looked up at her quizzically and said: 'Digging?'"

Joan Daniels of Siren, Wis.: "We had our granddaughters with us for our annual trip to the cemetery in preparation for Memorial Day. On the way, we explained where we were going and why.

"When we got there, the 5-year-old asked: 'Is this where my great-grandmother is planted?'"

Auntie Karen: "My niece Meredeth was about 3 or 4 years old when her great-grandmother died. Her mom and dad explained all about heaven to her and told her: 'That's where Great-grandma is now.'

"They arrived at the funeral home (which had the obligatory indirect lighting and soft music playing) shortly after this discussion and brought her up to us to say hello. Meredeth was gazing around with the most amazing look of awe upon her face when she reverently whispered: 'Is this heaven?'"

Ann of Fridley: "At Christmastime, one of my colleagues took his 5-year-old son to the cemetery to visit Grandpa's grave. It was the first time that the headstone was in place, with Grandpa's birth and death dates on it.

"The 5-year-old looked at the dates and said: 'Dad, is that Grandpa's telephone number in heaven?'"

Amy of Cottage Grove: "When my cousin was about 5 years old, our cousin Danny died, and everyone told him he was up in heaven now. A few months after that, Ryan's uncle on his dad's side of the family died, and when Ryan came home from school that day, his mom explained that his uncle had died and was probably up in heaven with Danny.

"Well, Ryan just looked at my aunt with disbelief and then, disgustedly, said to her: 'Well, Mom, he just got up there today. I don't think he's met him *yet*.'"

River Rat of Indian Point: "When my husband's nephew was staying at Grandma's one time and he was naughty, Grandma said if he wasn't good, he wouldn't go to heaven

"Junior said: 'I don't want to go to heaven. I want to go where Mama and Daddy go.'"

Holly of White Bear Lake: "Shelly, my 7-year-old, asked me if I would be in heaven when she got there. I said yes, and she said: 'Good! I want us to be together for the rest of our dead lives.'"

Joanie of South St. Paul: "As the mother of three, I was finally relaxing in the back yard one day, lying on the lounge chair, when my 5-year-old runs up to me and says: 'Mother, when you're dead and buried, way deep in the ground, we'll still love you and talk about you.'

"I could write a book on things this child has said to me. One day, we're sitting at the table—and she's totally convinced that the mother I have, who suffered a stroke three years ago, is not my true mother.

"I said to her: 'Yes, honey, Grammy is my mother—but when she became my mother, she did not have a stroke.'

"And she looked at me, in all of her wisdom, and said: 'My goodness, your heart must have just broke when she had the stroke.'

"And I said: 'Yes, honey, it did.'"

Gramma Judie of Stillwater: "Today, my almost-3-year-old granddaughter, Sara, and I were watching a video of her this past Easter. Sara was patting and kissing her only cousin, baby Zachary.

"Much to my family's despair, 3-month-old Zachary died of SIDS in June. Needless to say, the video was painful to watch and brought tears to my eyes.

"Little Sara asked my why I was sad and why I was crying. After my somewhat uncomplicated explanation about missing baby Zachary—but mentioning that someday we would be able to see him and play with him again in heaven—Sara replied in her sweet little voice: 'That's just the way it goes, Gramma.'

"Thank you, Lord, for my Sara."

Sandy of St. Paul: "I have a story to tell you about my niece, who lives on a country road in New Hampshire.

"Katie was 7 or 8 at the time, new to the area, and was riding the school bus daily past a small cemetery. After a few weeks of studying those headstones twice a day, Kate announced to her mother that she had figured out what R.I.P. stood for.

"When asked what that was, Katie proudly said: 'Return If Possible.'

"Love you, Kate."

Rose of Stillwater: "I just have a couple of cute things my little niece said to her grandpa as he lay dying.

"He'd been in the hospital and was very sick and sore, and she looked at him and said: 'Grandpa, I bet you wished you were a dad again, and not a grandpa.'

"Well, Grandpa passed away on Friday, and we had the visitation on Sunday and the funeral on Monday. We were all saying goodbye to Grandpa as he lay in the casket, and little granddaughter Karen— she's not even 6 years old yet—looked down at him and said: 'Goodbye, Grandpa! I'll see you in my mind.'

"Out of the mouths of babes come the best little answers to life and death."

About the Editor

The voice of Bulletin Board is Daniel Kelly, who created the column in 1990 and has edited it ever since. He also compiled the first two Bulletin Board books: *The Best of Bulletin Board* and *The Simple Pleasures.*

Almost everyone calls him Dan.

He is a native of Minnesota who graduated from Harvard College in 1975. Before coming to the *Saint Paul Pioneer Press,* he was editor of *Minnesota Monthly* and *Twin Cities* magazines.

He lives in Hopkins, Minnesota, with his wife and two daughters.

Other Pioneer Books You Can Order

The Simple Pleasures
This little volume is a compendium of life's simple pleasures—those small moments of beauty and satisfaction that light up the daily routine. $6.95 plus shipping and handling.

The Best of Bulletin Board
The human condition as seen by contributors to the popular *Pioneer Press* feature. Enjoy these extraordinary stories told by ordinary folks. $8.95 plus postage and handling.

Modern, Caring, Sensitive Male
Joe Soucheray, *St. Paul Pioneer Press* columnist, scrutinizes life in the '90s in the province of Minnesota. $9.95 plus shipping and handling.

Guide to Midwest Casinos
Where to wager in Illinois, Iowa, Minnesota, North Dakota, South Dakota and Wisconsin. $8.95 plus shipping and handling.

To order any Pioneer Press book, call (800) 642-6480.